SECRET SANTA

SECRET SANTA

This book is a work of fiction. Names, characters, places,
and incidents are the product of the author's imagination
or are used fictitiously. Any resemblance to actual events,
locales, or persons, living or dead, is coincidental.

Also by Kati Wilde

The Hellfire Riders Series

THE HELLFIRE RIDERS: SAXON & JENNY
THE HELLFIRE RIDERS: JACK & LILY
BREAKING IT ALL
GIVING IT ALL
CRAVING IT ALL
FAKING IT ALL
LOSING IT ALL

Christmas Romances

ALL HE WANTS FOR CHRISTMAS
THE WEDDING NIGHT
SECRET SANTA

Other Works

GOING NOWHERE FAST
BEAUTY IN SPRING
THE MIDWINTER MAIL-ORDER BRIDE
THE KING'S HORRIBLE BRIDE
HIGH MOON
THE MIDNIGHT BRIDE
PRETTY BRIDE
TEACHER'S PET WOLF
EVIL TWIN

KATI WILDE

ONE

Emma

"WELL, LOOK AT THAT." My new boss's bemused voice pulls my attention from the spreadsheet laid out on my computer screen. He's standing by the Christmas tree in front of the big window overlooking the office parking lot, his ever-present *World's #1 Dad* mug in hand. "It's snowing."

Dread tightens my stomach as I look out into the dark. It's the middle of December, so night comes early, and huge flakes are swirling through the halos of the streetlights. The pavement in the lot is already covered in white.

"Isn't that lovely!" Her huge belly leading the way, Marianne bustles in carrying a bright red Santa hat. "We might have a white Christmas after all."

A white, *freezing* Christmas. Oh joy.

"Maybe you better hold off on hoping for that," my boss says with a significant glance at her stomach. "You don't want to be driving to the hospital in a blizzard."

"And that's just like him, Emma." Marianne's pretty face is wreathed in a smile as she turns in my direction, so I drum up a weak smile in answer. "You'll say 'snow,' and a moment later, Bruce'll be thinking 'blizzard.' Or we'll run out of coffee pods, and a moment later he's dying of thirst. So you keep his head out of the doomsday clouds and you'll get on just fine."

My smile becomes more genuine then. I've only been working for Bruce Crenshaw for two weeks, but I've seen the older man's tendency to leap from the mundane to the dramatic in the space of a breath.

He winks at me, his faded blue eyes twinkling. "You'll notice that even though she's leaving me, I'm not crying that the sky is falling."

Marianne harrumphs. "You should have seen him last month, worrying we weren't ever going to find someone to fill my shoes. Yet here you are, Emma, and doing just… *oooh boy.*"

Flattening her hand to her stomach, she purses her lips and draws in a long, slow breath.

Bruce's face goes pale. "Did your water break?"

"Her tiny feet just gave my lungs a good kick." Rubbing her belly, Marianne awkwardly lowers into the seat facing my desk. "Maybe I shouldn't head over to the workshop right away, though. Do you mind running out there before you head to the bank, Emma?"

"Not at all." Pushing back my chair, I reach for my coat. It's only a denim jacket, hardly warm enough for the weather, but the dress code at this job runs to jeans and flannel so I've got a hoodie layered beneath it. "What do you need me to do?"

I'm being trained to step into Marianne's position as general office manager for Crenshaw's Custom Woodworks, which means that I'll pay the bills, take care of the payroll, and answer the phones. I won't have much reason to leave the small main office, and in the past two weeks I've only been to the workshop once—during the tour of the company on my first day, when the builders were out on a home installation.

Which is fine by me. Because one of the men in the shop unsettles my composure so badly, I'd rather avoid him.

Not that I have to put in much effort, since it seems as if he'd rather do anything than talk to me.

"Secret Santa," Marianne says, holding up the fuzzy red hat. "The guys each need to pick out a name. We'll be doing the gift exchange at the Christmas party."

Which is scheduled for next week—on the day before Christmas Eve, which is also Marianne's last day of work. I can't imagine how much of a party it will be, considering that only three people work in the office and four more in the shop, but if free food's available, I'm all in.

At the window, Bruce says, "Actually, Emma, it looks like my son's about to save you a trip. He's probably coming in to look over those new estimates. Marianne, will you sit in with us while we go over them? And when Logan heads back to the shop, he can take the Santa hat with him."

Nodding, she begins pushing up out of her chair. They start off toward Bruce's office, and for a long second I'm rooted to the spot, looking out the window at the man coming from the workshop on the opposite side of the parking lot.

Logan Crenshaw doesn't move like he's in a hurry, but his long strides are eating up the distance. Snowflakes glitter in his dark hair and dust his wide shoulders. He's not wearing a coat, just a faded red T-shirt that clings to his thick arms and broad chest, along with black jeans and steel-toed boots, but he doesn't seem to mind the cold, anyway. His face lifts to the sky as he walks, and through the dark his white grin flashes — as if in sheer pleasure at the sensation of the snowflakes drifting across his skin.

The sight of that grin sears something deep and unnamed inside me. Chest hurting, I turn away from the window and look blindly down at my desk.

I don't know why Logan Crenshaw affects me like he does. Well, part of it, I know. He's gorgeous. Rugged and masculine, with cheekbones as sharp as a knife's edge that could have been honed on the chiseled stone of his jaw. But whenever Logan comes into the office, he barely does more than grunt and growl his responses. And he looks at me as if... as if...

The truth is, I don't really know what to think of the way he looks at me, because I've never seen anything like it before.

He's got his dad's light blue eyes, but they're icier—and more intense. When he turns that glacial stare in my direction, I feel like the smallest, insignificant idiot who ever walked the earth. My tongue tangles up and internally I shrink like a mouse cornered by a snow leopard. A giant, gorgeous snow leopard.

But a mouse is *not* what I am. Not usually. It's just that when Logan's around, I can barely even squeak. And when Logan looks at me, he never grins—with pleasure or otherwise.

I think a part of me would give anything to be the one who made him smile like that.

It won't be today. Whatever enjoyment he found in the falling snow has darkened into a scowl by the time the office door swings open.

I catch that forbidding expression with a quick glance. And there goes the mouse inside me again, shriveling up into a tiny ball. My gaze immediately drops to the deposit slip on my desk, but I'm aware of Logan's every step as he comes closer. Neck aching with tension, I wait for him to pass by on the way to his dad's office.

But he stops in front of my desk. Heart thundering, I look up.

God, he's so big. The reception area where my desk sits isn't small, yet he threatens to overwhelm the space simply by standing there. It's not just his height—his dad is almost as tall—or the strength in his thick muscles, but the sheer *presence* of him. As if there's so much more to Logan than what I can see, and the magnitude of that unseen portion takes up all the room.

With snow melting in his dark hair, he stares down at me with that intense, unreadable gaze.

I'm not a mouse. I'm *not*. Forcing steel into my spine, I tell him, "Mr. Crenshaw is expecting you in his office."

Beneath straight black brows, those icy blue eyes narrow. His voice is a deep growl as he echoes, "'Mr. Crenshaw?'"

My cheeks heat. Now I sound like an uptight, mousy idiot. No one in this office is so formal. "Your dad."

Still scowling, he watches me for another long second, gaze slipping over my face. A muscle works in his jaw. Finally he nods and, without another word, heads for Bruce's office.

Immediately the tension gripping my body loosens, and I draw in a deep, shuddering breath. Every inch of my skin feels prickly, tight—and covered in gooseflesh as if I'd been running naked out in the snow.

As if I were cold. But I'm not. I'm burning, and my panties are so wet that if there was ever any ice inside me, it's long since melted.

Which is why Logan Crenshaw unsettles me so badly. Around him, I don't just transform into a tongue-tied little mouse. I become a tongue-tied little mouse with a drenched pussy.

I've never responded to *any* man this way—which is the reason I'm still a virgin at the age of twenty two. It's not that I've never noticed men, or never found them attractive. But from the moment I graduated high school and left my last foster home, trying to make a living always took priority, and I was too occupied with getting by to give more than a fleeting thought to sex.

I shouldn't be thinking of sex now, either. My priorities haven't changed. After being laid off from my last job and months of unemployment, I'm still just getting by. My overdue rent, my electric bill, my dying car—those are what I should be prioritizing. My body just hasn't gotten the message. Either that, or it's sending a message of its own.

Time to get laid, girly. Too bad it chose someone who scowls and growls at me instead of smiling and flirting.

Then again, maybe it's for the best. Screwing around isn't going to pay the bills. Neither is sitting here in sopping wet panties and staring blankly at a deposit slip, as if the form will fill itself out. With a sigh, I force myself to focus on work, and try to pretend that every cell within my body isn't attuned to the man sitting in Bruce's office.

I almost manage to convince myself. Still, when four-thirty rolls around and it's time to head to the bank, I drag my feet while collecting my coat and car keys. I need to knock on the office door to let them know I'm going. But poking my head in means Logan will probably scowl at me again, and then I'll be obsessing over his reaction all weekend—wondering what I ever did to deserve that response…and wondering why it hurts so much.

Too late, though. Because I've only just picked up my purse when the office door bangs open and Logan strides through, his icy gaze fixed on me.

He's looking pissed again, as if seeing me standing here irritates the hell out of him.

Why? What did I ever do?

My throat tight, I tear my gaze from his face and scoop up the deposit envelope. Marianne's right behind him, so even though my chest is aching, I force a chirpy, "I'm heading to the bank, unless there's anything else I need to do before taking off for the weekend."

Logan's deep growl answers me. "Have you picked a name yet?"

"A name?" I echo stupidly, because he's stopped right beside me. So close, I can smell him—the warm scent of pine and sawdust, deeper and warmer than the fragrance of the office's Christmas tree.

In response, he shoves the Santa hat under my nose.

For the Secret Santa gift exchange. Oh shit. My gaze darts past him to Marianne. "I'm not part of that this year, am I?"

"Of course you are, honey," she says brightly. "You're an employee of Crenshaw Woodworks now, aren't you?"

"So you already put my name in the hat?"

"I did."

"But…" I scramble for an excuse, trying not to stare

at the steely tendons flexing in Logan's forearm or his strong fingers crushing the hat's fuzzy white brim as he continues holding it out to me. "I barely know the other employees. I wouldn't know what anyone likes."

"Oh, everyone's easy. If you pick one of the guys' names, you just bring them a six pack of beer or make some cupcakes. Just something to celebrate the spirit of the season—and there's a ten-dollar limit, so no one's expecting anything fancy."

Except I don't have ten dollars to spare. I don't get my first paycheck until the thirty-first. Ten dollars means choosing between gas money or grocery money the last week of December. It means choosing between driving or eating.

And I need this job, so I'd probably choose driving.

Feeling sick to my stomach, I meet Logan's icy gaze—and only feel shittier when he grinds out, "I'm not going to bite you." He gives the hat a shake and the dangling white puffball swings wildly back and forth. "Just pick a fucking name."

Why is he so angry with me? Sparked by raging frustration, the timid mouse inside me burns to a crisp. I hiss at him, "I'm glad to see the spirit of the season has infused you with so much fucking patience" as I reach into the damn hat.

And oh my god. I thought his stare was intense before? I was wrong. *Now* the look he gives me pierces straight through my skin and sears me with a promise of...something.

Something that leaves me utterly frozen and helpless, tension riding my every muscle, my nerves on fire.

His gaze holding mine, Logan steps closer. His voice is a low rumble of gravel as he tells me, "You think I'm impatient, Emma? You have *no fucking idea* how patient I've been with you."

Why? What have I done? I search his face, but don't find an answer. My hand is buried in the velvet hat between us, and as he steps even closer, my senses are overwhelmed by his woodsy scent, his dominating size. Liquid desire pools deep inside me. If I don't get out of here, I'm going to dissolve into a puddle of arousal at his big, booted feet...where he would probably just scowl down at me.

I snatch a slip of paper out of the hat and flee.

TWO

Logan

I THINK IT'S REAL DAMN FUNNY that Emma Williams calls me impatient. She obviously doesn't know what the hell impatience looks like.

Is she sprawled across her desk with my face buried between her long, long legs?

No.

Is she on her knees with her golden hair tangled in my fist and with her pink lips wrapped around my thick cock?

No.

Is she crying out my name while I'm fucking her hard and deep? Is her hot pussy squeezing my dick when she comes all over me?

No.

None of that's happened yet. Even though there's been

nothing else in my head since I first laid eyes on her. So it seems to me I've been *real* fucking patient.

But my patience is coming to an end.

And it's all I can do not to tear after her when she races out the door. For some reason, she's been terrified of me since day one. At first I wondered if she was shy, but Emma doesn't have trouble meeting anyone else's eyes. She doesn't refuse to speak more than a few words to them. She doesn't tremble and blush when anyone else stands close to her. So it's me that's making her skittish, and chasing after her now won't help settle her down.

Hell if I'm not going to try changing that, though. Especially after she snapped at me, called me impatient. Whatever I'm doing that's scaring her, that flash of temper says she's starting to push back.

So I can finally push a bit harder.

Beginning with this. I shove my hand into the Santa hat and grab all the remaining names. Dumping the slips of paper onto the coffee table in the reception area, I shuffle through them. There's four names left. My dad, Marianne, and two guys from the shop—Patrick and Tyrone.

Shit. I look up. "Did you get Emma?"

Marianne stops fussing with the decorations on the Christmas tree and raises her brows at me. "If I tell you, it's not a *secret* Santa."

"Did you get her name?" Each word drops like a stone.

A lot of people scramble to fall in line when I use that

tone. Not Marianne. Her amused gaze skims the table, where the slips of paper are scattered around. "That's not how you're supposed to pick a name. You're supposed to trust in the magic of Christmas."

I do. But I also trust in the magic of capitalism. "I'll trade you a crib for Emma's name."

Which doesn't sound like much, except that Marianne knows I'm not talking about a crib that comes out of Babies"R"Us. My dad built a solid cabinetry and furniture business years ago, but in the past decade it's been my work that's put us on the map. Any custom piece I design and make, she can eventually sell for a small fortune or give to her kid as an heirloom.

A short battle plays out on her face. Finally she sighs, a sound filled with deep regret. "I can't trade hers because I got someone else's name."

Which leaves only two people who might have gotten Emma's. "You think she picked out her own?"

And ran off before she even looked at it.

Lips pursed, Marianne regards me silently for a long second—then gives a small shake of her head.

So my dad got Emma's name. Fuck yeah. I can work with that.

I pocket Marianne's name and sweep the others back into the hat. And because she looks so damn disappointed, I tell her, "Don't you give up hope on that crib."

Especially considering I've got a completed nursery set sitting in my workshop at home—a present to

Marianne from me and my dad, for putting up with us the past ten years.

Laughing, she wags an admonishing finger at me. "Don't you ruin my holiday surprise, Logan Crenshaw."

"I won't." But maybe she'll be willing to trade something else—such as information. "Did Emma say anything that explains why she's so damn scared of me?"

Marianne doesn't even blink, or try to claim that Emma isn't afraid. So she's noticed it, too. But she shakes her head. "Not a word."

Fuck.

So what is it, then? Is it my that size terrifies her? I'm a big man, but that's not going to change anytime soon.

And when I get her tight little body under mine, she's going to love how big I am.

If I get her under me. Frustrated as hell, I rake a hand through my hair. It's a bit long. I don't bother shaving every day so my jaw's got some scruff. Not enough to scare off a woman, I don't think. It never has before. But that was then, and none of those women matter now.

Only Emma does.

"Although…" Marianne draws out the word as far as it can go before continuing, "It might be the way you look at her."

I frown. "How do I look at her?"

"Like you're a raging bull moose in rutting season."

That's pretty fucking accurate. But I didn't realize it showed.

Marianne isn't done, though. "And when you look at her, the air around you is combustible. I sometimes think the only reason everyone in the vicinity doesn't spontaneously become pregnant is because they're all men. And because my husband already knocked me up."

Shit. So Emma probably sees that I'm a walking hard-on. But what am I supposed to do different? *Not* looking at her isn't an option. Neither is toning it down.

Hell, I thought I *was* toning it down.

But it doesn't matter. Failing isn't an option, either. "All right. Thanks. I'll work it out."

"Well, hurry up about it," is her cheeky reply. "Because I want to see this happen before I'm gone."

I do, too.

Santa hat in hand, I head outside. The snow's still falling. Everything's quiet in parking lot. Only a single set of footprints are visible through the snow. Emma's. My gaze follows them to the spot by the fence, where she's been parking her ancient Toyota. Her car should be gone.

It's not.

The streetlight's shining through her windshield, giving me a good look inside Emma's car. She's leaning forward in the driver's seat with her elbows braced against her steering wheel and her face buried in her hands.

I know that posture. It's the universal sign for *'Why the hell won't my stupid fucking engine start?'*

Bad luck for her. Merry Christmas to me.

Boots crunching in the snow, I stalk across the lot.

She doesn't look up until I rap my knuckles against her window. Her head jerks back and her gaze flies to mine.

And a second later I'm laid out, just fucking laid out. Physically still standing upright, but internally flattened by a one-two punch.

The first blow comes when I see the glitter of tears in her big brown eyes, glistening drops that magnify a soul-deep despair.

But it's the second blow that's the hardest. Because in the next moment she blinks and a smile curves her full lips. And although her eyes are still overly bright, there's barely a sign that anything's wrong as she begins cranking down the window.

Beautiful though it is, that smile's all wrong—because she's never aimed one at me before. And her tears squeeze at my chest, but this brave face she puts up is a kick to my heart. Because that brave face…that's armor.

This woman's a fighter. Someone who's been knocked down—maybe more than once. But who always gets up, straps on her shields, and keeps going.

And I wanted Emma before this moment. From the day I first met her, I wanted her in my bed, and a whole lot more.

Now I'm sure I *need* her.

She's still wearing that friendly, bright smile as the window comes down. Her cheeks and nose are pink from the cold or from crying. "Do you need help with something?"

"By the looks of it, I'm not the one who needs help." My voice is rougher than I intend, but this woman just knocked something loose in me. Though I'm dying to know what's hurting her—dying to fix it and take that hurt away—she obviously doesn't want to expose her vulnerabilities. Demanding answers might make her more scared of me than she already is. "Did you leave your headlights on?"

"No. My battery just doesn't like the cold." As if the gesture's part of the explanation, she waves a hand toward the passenger side, where a pair of jumper cables lies coiled on the seat.

I frown. That's not where people usually store their jumper cables. "This happens often?"

She shrugs. "I usually just have to get a jump from my neighbor in the mornings. Then in the afternoon it starts okay. Except for today."

Because the temperature dropped. But it's not getting warmer anytime soon. "Sounds like you need a new battery."

"I guess I do." Her smile becomes brighter, tighter—as if she's putting up another layer of armor between me and whatever put those tears of despair in her eyes earlier. "Do you mind giving me a jump so I can get to the bank before it closes?"

"I could, but unless you're driving for a while, a jump will only get you as far as the next time you turn off the car."

"That's fine. The bank has a drive-thru. I won't need to stop until I get home."

"And if your engine stalls? You'll be sitting dead. So I've got a better idea." One that'll keep her near me for a while. "I'll get Patrick out here to hook up the battery charger that's sitting in the shop, then I'll give you a ride to the bank in my rig. By the time we come back, you should have enough juice for a couple of starts."

Tonight, at least. Most likely it'll be dead again by morning. But I'll take care of that soon enough.

She hesitates, her gaze searching my face before looking past me—toward the office. Weighing her fear of me against the fear of making a bad impression at her new job, I'm guessing.

Neither my dad nor Marianne would give a shit if she didn't make that deposit until Monday. I won't point that out, though.

"You don't mind?" she finally asks.

Mind helping her out? That doesn't even merit an answer.

"Pop your hood so Patrick can connect the charger," I tell her. "I'll bring my truck around."

A few minutes later, I've got Emma Williams sitting in my cab, holding out her ungloved hands to the blast of the heater. She's withdrawn into herself again, avoiding my eyes—maybe afraid that I'll drag her across the bench seat and fuck her hard and deep.

But I won't do that. I'm just thinking it.

The doing can come later.

"Thank you again," she says softly.

"Yup."

A short answer, but I'm trying hard not to fall into rutting bull moose mode. Not easy, considering that my cock's a steel spike lodged behind my zipper — and considering that Emma's only an arm's length away, eyes bright and her armor in place. Christ, but she's a sight. That long, just-been-fucked blond hair. Those big brown eyes and a sweet short nose over succulent pink lips that have featured in every fantasy since I've met her. Those lips and those legs. They're a mile-fucking-long, though she's not that tall. Average height, maybe. She's wearing jeans now, denim hugging her sweet thighs and calves and cupping her ass the way I'd love to. First time I saw her, she was wearing a short pleated skirt over dark tights, and I've been picturing those leanly muscled legs wrapped around my waist ever since.

Around my waist, or around my head. Don't much care as long as her thighs are squeezing me tight as she comes.

But I keep the rutting bull reined in, even though I can feel her stealing glances in my direction. I'm guessing she won't look at me if I'm looking back so I keep my eyes on the road, instead.

But it's killing me not to see her pretty face. At the first intersection, I glance over. She's watching me, her plump bottom lip trapped between her teeth as if she's got something to ask but uncertain whether she should.

Emma Williams shouldn't ever feel uncertain around me. I narrow my eyes. "What?"

Maybe that was too blunt, because her hesitation seems to deepen. But only for a second.

Then her eyes narrow right back. "Did you really drop out of high school when you were fifteen?"

There's no question where she got that. "You read that piece in *Northwest Quarterly?*"

A regional magazine, which currently has my face staring out from the cover in the checkout aisle of every local grocery store. It's not the first time I've been featured in industry and small business magazines, and probably won't be the last. Because as much as I hate those interviews, they're good for the company. In this latest one, the photographer posed me in front of a black walnut armoire I'd just finished, then caught me grinning at some point during the shoot, and the overall effect could be called *Smug Dickhead in a Flannel Shirt.* Then the headline reads, "At fifteen, he's a high school dropout; at twenty six, he's schooling the woodworking masters."

Which is bullshit. I've done well for the company, made a name for myself. But I'm sure as hell not schooling any masters.

It's all right if Emma thinks I am, though. And I especially like the thought of her being curious enough to read about me. God knows if she was on the cover of a magazine, I'd snatch up any information I could about her.

Then stroke my cock raw while looking at her photo.

But she shakes her head. "I only saw the cover when I was at the library. Someone else was reading the magazine, though, so I didn't get a chance to look at the article."

"Ask Dad or Marianne for a copy. There should be a couple lying around." Because my dad bought a whole stack of them when the edition first came out in November—and the more Emma knows about me, the faster she'll realize she doesn't need to be afraid. And I still haven't answered her question. "Anyway, it's true. I left school early. But what the article doesn't say is that it was done with state approval, as kind of a homeschool arrangement. I spent the next year in apprenticeships and got my GED as soon as I could test for it. Those write-ups always use the dropout angle, though."

They have since the beginning—which was when HGTV produced a season-long show following a celebrity renovating her house. They added segments featuring the architects, the construction crews, and the artisans involved, so when they discovered the actress picked out a dining set that was designed and built by a teenager, they were all over it. We got fifteen minutes of national airtime, complete with a heart-tugging interview with my dad, tears in his eyes and choking up while he talked about how we lost my mom in a car accident when I was eight. By the end of it, they had me looking like a woodworking prodigy who'd arisen from the ashes of tragedy.

As slanted as it all was, I'm not complaining. After that show aired, we could barely keep up with the orders. Now we have two sides to the business: the custom shop, that's me and the guys. And my dad's side, which is the production of our catalog items—all off site and basically like a furniture assembly line.

That original story slanted every interview afterward, though, and the dropout label is brought up every time. But I get it. A 'loser makes good' headline probably sells more copies than 'asshole studies his craft and works his ass off—and is lucky enough to sell a piece to a high-profile buyer and capitalize on the wave of publicity that follows—then over the course of ten years takes his dad's already solid business to the next level.'

Emma's eyes are alight with interest. "So you didn't flunk out. It was more like you weren't going to waste your time doing anything else."

"That's exactly what it was like." I practically grew up in my dad's shop. Officially I wasn't an employee until I was sixteen, but I was in there designing and building long before that. I didn't see any reason to spend more time in school when the stuff I wanted to learn was outside of it.

"You were that sure at fifteen?"

"I was that sure at five."

Her dark blond eyebrows arch in disbelief.

It's true, though. "When something's right for me, I know it," I tell her.

The same way I know Emma's right for me.

I don't think she's ready to hear that, though. And maybe it's the way I'm looking at her, but she bites her lip again and averts her face, squirming in her seat as if she's itching to escape.

So I ease up. "But it wasn't just me. You've probably seen already how my dad always jumps right to the worst, yeah? He worries about everything." At her nod, I continue, "When I told him that I wanted to leave school, he didn't have a single doubt. He knew it was right for me, too. And he says I get that certainty from my mom, because she was the same way. She knew exactly what she wanted and she didn't waste time pursuing it."

Her career, my dad. My mom proposed to him a week after meeting him, so I'm already trailing behind her. I don't suppose my dad was afraid of her, though. Not considering that I was born nine months after they met.

Chances are I won't move as fast as she did with a kid, either. I'd like a few years with Emma to myself.

And although I'm glad she asked about me, I'm ready to talk about her. "What about you?"

She shrugs. "I finished high school."

Then went to the local community college to study business and accounting, all the while working part time as a bank teller and part time as a file clerk at an accounting firm. She got her associates degree and started a full time job bookkeeping at a construction firm, until it went under a while back.

"I've seen your résumé," I tell her, but I don't add that I only pulled it out of the filing cabinet after I met her. My dad and Marianne handled the hiring. "I'm asking whether managing an office is always what you wanted to do."

"Oh." She blinks. "Yes, it is. I didn't imagine Crenshaw's, specifically, but this kind of work."

I love that answer. Not sure I believe it, but I love it. Because I don't want her moving on to another job anytime soon. "Really?"

She nods. "Maybe not the part where I answer phones, but the accounting part of it."

Marianne's the opposite. She puts up with the book-keeping because it's part of the job. But she loves inter-acting with people.

"So you like the numbers?"

"Not the numbers themselves, exactly, but the way they add up in a ledger. The way they all make sense." Her voice softens with a note of utter satisfaction, just as I imagine her sighs might sound when she's lying against me, sweaty and exhausted and her pussy juices still coating my dick. "I love how the assets and the liabilities equal each other, and that, no matter how many expenses go out and how much income comes in, there's always a credit for every debit—and a debit for every credit. The way it all fits together just…appeals to me on every level."

"I've never heard anyone talk about accounting like that." Jesus. It's sexy as fuck.

So is the blush that climbs her cheeks. "It's just that balance sheets are simple," she says, "no matter how complicated the accounting itself gets. And the math is never as complicated as people are."

"People are simple."

She gives me a look that says I'm crazy.

"Take me, for example," I tell her. "All I want out of life is football in the winter, barbecues in the summer — and beer to drink with both. Add in work for my hands and the love of a good woman, and I'm set for life."

And if I could only have one, I'd take the woman and give up everything else.

But only if that woman is Emma.

A little smile curves her lips. "All right," she concedes. "Maybe I said it wrong. *People* can be simple. But the relationships between them usually aren't."

I won't argue with that. Though it makes me wonder how complicated her relationships have been that she takes such pleasure in a balance sheet. It also might explain why she's so damn scared of me — maybe she senses what I want from her isn't simple at all.

Aside from when we're fucking. That'll be real simple. So I'll start with sex before easing her into the complicated shit, like living together and marriage and babies.

Except she's fidgeting again, face averted and squirming a little in her seat, so I'll have to hold off on the fucking, too. Until she's not so jumpy around me.

And start with something even simpler. "What do you want for your Secret Santa gift?"

Her head swings around, that long golden hair tumbling over her shoulder in thick waves, her eyes wide. "You picked my name? Well, I'm easy. Just don't get me anything."

Like that'll happen. "I didn't get your name. My dad did."

"Tell him the same thing, then. Tell him he doesn't need to get me anything."

"Yeah, you don't know my dad. If he gets you nothing—or the wrong thing—he'll spend the next few months worrying that you're offended and planning to quit."

Her brow furrows. "I wouldn't do that."

"Try telling him that," I say dryly. "He'll worry anyway. But if I mention to him that I overheard you saying that you want…?" I leave that open, hoping she'll fill that in. But when she remains quiet, I continue, "If I can tell him what to get you, he'll stop worrying that he'll give the wrong thing."

"Oh," she says softly.

"So what do you want? If you could have anything."

My answer's easy. I want Emma.

It's apparently a harder question for her. She bites her lip again, and I glimpse naked yearning in her eyes before she faces forward, looking out the windshield.

After a long minute she says slowly, "Maybe a pair of pine scented candles? The tree in the office smells so good. It'd be nice to smell that at my apartment, too."

The bank's coming up across the street. I slow the truck and wait for a break in traffic. "Because you've got one of those artificial trees?"

"I don't have any tree," she says, and as a wood man, I can't decide if that's better or worse than having an artificial one. "It's just me at home."

It's just me at home, too, but I've got two trees — one in my bedroom and one downstairs — and both are fully decked out.

I enjoy the hell out of Christmas. Hell, being the simple man that I am, I enjoy *every* day. But especially this one, since Emma ended up in my truck.

I cross the lane, pulling into the bank's lot. "So I should tell him that you want your place to smell like a Christmas tree."

"Yes." She hands over the deposit envelope as I drive up to the teller window, then a moment later she's looking past me with a gorgeous smile widening her lips. "Hey, Traci."

"Emma!" The teller on the opposite side of the window clunks open the metal drawer. "How are you doing, girl?"

"Good." Emma glances at me. "I finally got a new job."

"Mmm-hmm," is the skeptical reply through the speaker. "Well, he does look like a lot of work."

Emma's cheeks burst with color, but her laugh is light and easy. "No, really. Logan Crenshaw, this is Traci. We used to work here together when I was a teller. Traci, Logan is one of my new bosses."

Oh *hell* no. If I'm Emma's boss, then everything I plan to do to her becomes some fucked up sexual harassment shit. She likes things to be simple and that would *not* be simple. Or ethical.

Frowning, I shake my head. "Not a boss. Just an

employee. My dad owns the place. I don't."

Emma looks at Traci again and they exchange one of those glances that women do, a flaring of their eyes that seems to contain an entire conversation.

Then Emma says, "How are your boys?"

"Texting complaints every minute since it began snowing."

A little frown pleats her brow. "But don't they like the snow?"

"They love it. They're just upset because it started after school let out. So they're complaining that the universe cheated them out of a snow day." Traci huffs out a laugh, her long nails tapping rapidly at her keyboard. "And me, I'm thinking, 'Hallelujah!' No need to arrange for a sitter."

"A Christmas miracle just for you." Emma grins. "Are you doing anything special for the holiday?"

"Not a thing. Just my parents and my sister coming over. You?"

Emma shakes her head.

"Well, give me a call if you want to join us. You know there's always a seat at our table for you. And here's your receipt, Mr. Bossman."

"Thanks," I say gruffly and reach for the slip. "Nice meeting you, Traci."

"You, too." She looks past me at Emma and winks. "Enjoy your new job, hon. And every time you make a deposit, make sure you come to my window to tell me about it."

"I will." Emma's face is pink again. "I'll see you soon."

She falls quiet as I drive forward, my jaw clenched against boiling frustration. Because she claims relationships are difficult and she prefers balance sheets to personal interactions. Yet here she is, sweet and funny and obviously on easy and friendly terms with this woman. Just as I've seen her be with Marianne and my dad.

But not me.

I feel her studying my profile, and there's another of those maddening hesitations before she says, "Traci didn't mean anything by any of that, you know."

I shoot her a sharp glance. "Any of what?"

"Nothing," she whispers and turns her face away from me again.

Goddammit. "Why are you so fucking scared of me?"

Her head whips around, eyes wide. "What?"

"You. Scared." My fingers tighten on the steering wheel. "Of me."

"I'm not!"

"Bullshit. Then why are you always shrinking away from me?"

"Because you're always growling at me!" she shoots back. "And I don't know what I did to piss you off!"

That surprises the shit out of me. "You think I'm angry?"

Her eyebrows abruptly draw together, as if she's as surprised as I am. "Aren't you?"

"No."

She eyes me warily. "You look like you are."

"That's just my face." My *I'm going to fuck you good and hard* face. Which she ought to get used to, since I'm not sure I can look at her any other way. "I'm not pissed."

"Oh." It's a soft realization, and I see some of the tension in her posture fade as her gaze searches mine — as if recalibrating what she thought my expression meant.

And she thought I was angry. All this time. Marianne saw a rutting bull moose, but she knows me well. Emma doesn't.

But now we can start over. "All right?"

"Yeah." Then her brows arch and she gives me a little smile. "Though now I'd hate to see how scary you look when you *are* angry."

"It doesn't happen a lot." Frustrated, yes. Angry, no. And this time with her is too damn short. We're only a few minutes away from the office and I'm not ready to give her up yet. "Is there anywhere else you need to stop before we head back to your car?"

Pressing her lips together, she shakes her head.

Shit. "The longer your battery is hooked up, the more it'll charge."

"That's okay. I just need it to start."

"We could stop at Murphy's, kill some time over a few drinks."

She hesitates again, but this time I know fear of me isn't causing that uncertainty. And that sweet yearning touches her face, as if she'd like to go.

But she says, "I shouldn't."

"You got something better to do? You said you were heading straight home."

"I am."

"So you've got someone coming over or picking you up for a date?" It's Friday night. No way she made it through this week without someone asking her out.

Shaking her head, she laughs as if me asking that was a joke instead of the deadly serious question I meant it as.

"Then come out with me," I tell her.

Again that yearning. Again she shakes her head. "I really can't."

"Why?" I'm pushing hard, I know it. Maybe too hard. Because I can see that armor go up.

Tearing her gaze from mine, she slowly says, "Well, I've got a new battery to buy."

Ah. Little Miss Balance Sheet. I bet she budgets every expense for months — and she was out of work for a while, so her budget probably looks pretty damn thin.

"My treat," I tell her.

Still she shakes her head. "I don't know when I can pay you back."

"Pay me back?" That frustration rears up hot and hard again. "A treat doesn't go into a balance sheet."

The look she gives me says she doesn't believe that for a second.

And then there's nothing left to say. Because she's withdrawing again, going quiet in the passenger seat. Not in fear, but just…pulling away from me.

Fuck.

If I push now, she's just going to withdraw further. So I'll back off tonight. But I'm not giving up. I'll simply find another way to get beneath her armor. I just need an *in*.

And thanks to a name and a Santa hat, I've already got one.

THREE

Emma

SATURDAY MORNING, I WAKE UP buried under my mound of blankets and lie there for a while, my mood strangely buoyant. I don't realize why until after my quick shower, when I'm scrubbing a towel over my shivering skin.

The heavy knot of anxiety in my stomach is gone.

It shouldn't be. My apartment's freezing because I've been staying one partial payment ahead of the electric company's cutoff notice for months, and to keep the bill manageable I don't set the thermostat above fifty five. And last night after I drove home, I added the expense of a car battery to the spreadsheet I use to calculate my budget. When I was hired at Crenshaw's, putting in my anticipated income was an enormous relief, but many of the columns still remained in the red until June. With the purchase of a battery, the red will creep into July.

But Logan Crenshaw isn't angry with me.

When I head outside, my car doesn't start. I don't expect it to, really, but last night in the parking lot when I turned the key and my dash indicators didn't even light up, months of despair and worry crashed in on me in an overwhelming rush. This morning, that dead battery doesn't seem so dire. It just needs to last two more weeks, and jumping it each morning has worked well so far. When I'm at work, I can ask them to hook up that charger again. That'll get me to and from the office until the end of the month.

And Logan's not angry. He just looks that way.

That shouldn't matter so much. When I weigh Logan's not-anger against those red columns, that anxiety should still be chewing at my gut.

It's not, though. Instead I feel hopeful as I start off through the snow. The best thing about my apartment — aside from my awesome landlord who let me pay only half my rent this month on the promise to settle the balance out of my first paycheck — is that the location is within walking distance of everything I need. So I spend a few hours at the wonderfully heated library, then walk to the grocery store armed with its weekly ad flyer. I don't buy anything. Instead I head to the bakery aisle and try to figure out how I'm going to afford a dozen cupcakes.

I work it all out back at home, sitting on my sofa

wearing a stocking cap, fingerless gloves, my heaviest sweater, and a blanket tucked around my legs. My back is wedged up against the sofa arm, because my ancient laptop battery doesn't hold a charge any better than my car battery does, and whoever designed this apartment put only one outlet in the living room—and in the most inconvenient possible spot—so I've got my adaptor cord strung across the floor in a taut line from outlet to couch. But I'm cozy warm because the laptop is like a heating pad on my thighs, I've got a peanut butter sandwich filling my stomach, and I'm no longer dreading the gift exchange so much.

This Secret Santa thing might turn out okay, after all.

Buying store-made cupcakes would be cheaper than making them—only five dollars versus eight dollars for a cake mix, chocolate frosting, a dozen eggs, and cupcake liners. But the mix only calls for three eggs, which means I'd have nine left at home. Plus it yields two dozen cupcakes, so after giving half away, I could eat the remaining cupcakes for breakfast or lunch. Add a bag of potatoes and I'm set for next week.

Not exactly healthy, but I can make up for that when all those red columns are in the black.

I'm already dreaming of hashbrowns and eggs on Christmas morning as I put away my laptop and grab one of the paperbacks I picked up at the library—*The Martian*. It's a re-read, my third time through in as many years, because its such ridiculous fun.

And compared to growing potatoes in human feces while stranded on an alien planet, those red columns don't seem so bad.

That red won't last forever, either. Only seven more months of pinching every single penny and barely keeping my head above water. Then I'll catch up on all of my payments and those columns will be in the black.

And Logan isn't angry. He's just absurdly sexy.

Maybe next time—when those columns are in the black—I can go out for that drink. If there is a next time. He's not angry, but my answer yesterday didn't make him happy, either. So maybe he won't ever suggest it again.

My chest suddenly aching, I settle deeper into my sofa cushions—then almost jump out of my skin when someone pounds on my front door.

Holy crap. Someone's got a huge fist. And I'm not expecting anyone—I rarely have visitors—but I suppose it's not too late for a delivery. Not that I've ordered anything. But I can't imagine any of my neighbors or friends banging on the door like that. The UPS guy, though, maybe he would.

I throw the blanket from my lap and the skin on my thighs immediately goosebumps in the cold air. I'm not completely bare, though—I've got on flannel sleep shorts and striped knee-high socks—and my sweater is long enough that I could belt it and wear it as a dress. With my hat and gloves, I probably look like a complete dork, but…that's pretty accurate. And I'm sure the UPS guy won't care.

Book still in hand, I go up on tiptoe to look through the peephole.

No one's there.

My apartment building is basically two buildings separated by a breezeway that leads to the parking lot. Through the fisheye lens I can see the unit doors across from mine, along with most of the breezeway. It's all empty. With my security chain connected, I open the door.

A small white gift box sits on my step, topped by an envelope with OPEN ME NOW, EMMA scrawled across the front in thick black marker.

Weird. But okay.

The box is light. I rip open the envelope. There's a typed note inside—on Crenshaw Woodwork's letterhead. So this isn't some random gift drop. It's starting to make more sense. But only a little. Because the message is:

> *Open the box and find your first gift.*
> *Put it on.*
> *Unlock your door and wait.*
> *Don't remove your gift until I'm gone.*
> *Signed,*
> YOUR SECRET SANTA

The signature is scrawled in the same thick marker. Then there's another little handwritten note, a TRUST ME, EMMA with an arrow pointing to the logo on the letterhead.

Because I'll be unlocking my door so that someone can come in. He's trying to reassure me that I'll be safe.

He won't be a stranger. I know my Secret Santa is Bruce Crenshaw. Logan told me he was.

Logan was also supposed to tell his dad to give me pine-scented candles...and the gift exchange is supposed to take place during the Christmas party. We're not at the Christmas party, and the gift isn't heavy enough to be candles. Unless they're tea lights.

My breath stops when I open the little box.

A blindfold. Or more accurately, a sleep mask — one that Santa might wear, made from red satin and trimmed with white fur. But since I won't be sleeping, the intended purpose is the same as a blindfold's.

So I'm supposed to cover my eyes and let Bruce come in? The note seems to suggest he'll quickly go, and the blindfold is just so that I won't know who he is.

So he must be bringing something in, then leaving it here. And although I'm hesitant...I'm also *so* curious. I'm charmed by all of it, too. I like Bruce. He's so sweet — and he's apparently taking this Secret Santa thing to another level. And no one's *ever* put this much effort into a gift for me before.

And, okay — this is the most exciting thing that's happened to me in a very long time. Which is sad. But there it is.

I leave the door open a few inches. Backing up against the wall so I'm out of the way, I take a deep breath.

And put on the mask.

I have to pull off my stocking cap to fit the elastic

strap over my head. As soon as I tug the satin into place, every sensation seems to sharpen.

The prickle of the cold against my thighs. The softness of the mask's furred trim against my cheeks. The rapid thundering of my heart.

And from the breezeway, the approaching tread of boots on concrete.

A shiver works over my skin. Not cold. Not really. It's just that my head is trying to make up for the blindfold, and I'm imagining what I can't see.

But I'm not imagining Bruce. I'm imagining Logan.

It's because of that tread. The unhurried pace of it. Logan moves like that, his stride slow and long, as if he's never in a rush to do anything. I've noticed it so many times.

Maybe Bruce does, too, though. My impression is that when he walks, he's quicker and more focused. But the truth is…I haven't paid as much attention to Bruce as I have his son.

So I try to adjust my mental picture. I try to imagine Bruce's lean height and his salt-and-pepper hair and his easy smile.

But when my hinges softly squeak, I imagine Logan's dark scowl, instead. I imagine his broad frame filling my open door. I imagine him spotting me standing here, my back pressed against the wall, my hair in a thick messy braid, wearing a satin mask and knee-high socks and with my breath skimming quickly through my parted lips.

He wouldn't be able to see the hardening of my nipples through my thick sweater. He wouldn't be able to see my pussy flooding my panties.

Oh my god. I'm so turned on.

My face heats. Beneath the mask, I squeeze my eyes tightly closed, as if to shut out the mental picture of Logan watching me with that icy gaze. But it's not Logan, it's his dad. I'm getting hot while my poor unsuspecting boss is standing right there.

Luckily, Bruce can't see my arousal. He has no idea what's going on in my head.

And I have no idea what he's bringing in. There's a strange brushing sound, as if he swept the stiff bristles of a huge broom across the side of the door frame.

I'm still puzzling over that noise as he takes the first few steps inside, then the strong scent of fresh pine hits me and all at once I know what the sound was.

Branches. From a Christmas tree.

A *real* Christmas tree.

A burning lump fills my throat. Behind the mask, my eyes squeeze shut again, trying to stop the tears that threaten to burst free, but I can't stop the soft sobbing breath that shudders from my chest.

I don't think he hears it. His boots are still crossing the room, then he pauses for a moment. Maybe deciding where to put it. Maybe looking for an outlet so that I can plug in the lights.

I don't have lights. But it doesn't matter. Already my

apartment smells *so* good, and this is going to be the best Christmas ever.

My throat aching with sweet tears, I whisper, "The outlet's over in that wall nook," and point a trembling finger in that direction. "Just follow the computer cord."

A moment later comes a soft *thunk* as he sets the tree down. I think he fiddles with its position a couple of times, because I hear the scrape of pine needles against coarse fabric, as if he's reaching in between the branches to adjust the rotation of the trunk.

Finally he starts heading back my way. Leaving.

"Thank you." My voice is thick. "You must have spent much more than a Secret Santa was supposed to, but—"

"You're going to take it anyway."

My breath stops. That gravelly voice doesn't belong to Bruce.

It belongs to his son.

And Logan's not heading for the door. Everything inside me draws up tight and hot as his footsteps come nearer. I can't see him, but I know he's right in front of me. I can feel his warmth and his breath, and there's a soft thump against the wall—as if he's braced his hands beside my head so that he can lean in, and I think our gazes would be level if a mask wasn't covering my eyes.

"You're going to take it, Emma." Low and rough, he moves in closer, until his mouth can't be more than a few inches from mine. "Aren't you?"

I am. He'd have to fight me to get that tree out of my

apartment again. Even though— "I shouldn't. It's too much. We have a ten-dollar limit."

His growl deepens. "Didn't your parents ever teach you not to haggle over the cost of a gift?"

"No," I respond breathlessly, my heart racing. "They dumped me on the front steps of a church just after I was born."

Utter silence.

Then he says, "You ever shove your foot so deep into your mouth that you can just about feel your toes tickle your prostate?"

Giggling, I shake my head.

"Well, my foot's that deep right now. I'm sorry, Emma. I didn't know."

"It's okay." It really is. I never knew my parents, so I can miss the *idea* of them, but I don't miss them. Whereas Logan lost a mother he knew and loved. "Probably better to be raised in foster care the way I was than by someone who couldn't keep me."

"I don't know about that." His voice is a low rumble again, but lighter. Teasing. "Because your foster parents didn't teach you that you're supposed to accept a gift without questioning the cost."

"Yeah," I sigh. "Some of my foster families made certain I was aware of *exactly* how much a gift costs."

"So they put them on a balance sheet." Not so teasing now.

I shrug. "I can't complain. They mostly all treated me

well."

There's a long pause, filled with his heavy exhalation, as if he's struggling to control his reaction to that. Maybe it's a response to the *mostly*.

Or maybe he doesn't like the balance sheet. He didn't yesterday when I turned him down for that drink. But it helps me make certain I'm not asking too much of anyone—or leeching off anyone. And when it comes to money and friends, I *really* don't like it when my columns are in the red.

I don't know if Logan is a friend. But I absolutely do not want to start off in the red with him.

"I just like it equal," I whisper when his silence continues. "And with the Secret Santa, that dollar limit makes it all equal."

Or as much as it can be. Some gifts are more thoughtful, chosen with the specific person in mind. Some people spend more time on theirs, decorating or creating their gift. But in monetary value, at least, they're fairly even.

"All right," he says gruffly. "So you're fretting over the difference between ten dollars and the cost of that tree. Well, then—you just make up the difference."

Familiar anxiety knots my gut. "Okay. But it'll take me a little while to pay you back."

"I didn't say it'd be with money."

That makes no sense. "Logan—"

"Who the hell is this *Logan* asshole?" His voice is low and amused. "I'm your Secret Santa. Call me Santa."

I can't stop another giggle. "Santa."

"See? You don't owe *Logan* anything. But Santa's wondering how many kisses it will take to make up that difference."

My heart stutters. "Kisses?"

"The long and deep kind." It's a guttural confirmation. "As if my mouth's slowly fucking yours."

His mouth fucking mine.

Slowly.

Oh god. Everything inside me is shaking, my brain barely functioning. I feel him shift closer, as if he's no longer leaning over me with his hands braced against the wall, but as if he's straightened again and the entire length of his body is only inches from mine.

Big, warm palms cup my jaw and gently tilt my head back, as if he's looking down at my face. Callused thumbs slide along the bottom edge of the mask. "How many kisses, Emma?"

My body trembling, I manage to stumble into an answer. "I–It depends on what value you'd assign to a kiss."

I'd give mine for free and never make up the difference.

Voice pure gravel, he replies, "Emma Williams, I'd bring you a thousand trees for just one taste of your lips."

A nervous huff of laughter escapes me, though he didn't say anything funny. It's just that what he *did* say has my mind spinning and my synapses misfiring and I can't control anything coming out of my mouth. "Then I suppose the tree you brought is worth one thousandth of one kiss. So I could make up the difference with a little peck."

"A little peck? Fuck that math," he growls, sounding like every time I thought he was angry with me. Hard and rough and abrupt.

But it's not anger.

Instead it's sweet and hot. And so soft, when his firm lips settle against mine. Lightly he teases the width of my upper lip with butterfly kisses before catching my bottom lip gently between his teeth. Erotic delight shivers through me. My mouth opens on a shuddering breath and he licks his way inside, his tongue tasting mine in a leisurely, sensual slide.

And slowly, so slowly, his mouth begins fucking mine.

There's no other word for what he's doing. I've never fucked anyone, and I've only kissed a few people, but those kisses were nothing like this. With every slow thrust of his tongue, Logan takes complete possession of my lips, his big hands cradling my cheeks as he angles me for a deeper taste, his chin rasping lightly against mine. His jaw is smooth, smoother than my mind pictured when I imagined him coming through the door, because only yesterday thick stubble shadowed his face.

As if he shaved just before coming. As if he had every intention of kissing me when he got here and didn't want to rip up my skin.

And the thought that this was part of a plan—that he made this effort just to kiss me—makes it all even hotter.

On a soft moan, I rise up higher on my toes, my arms wreathing his neck. The fingers of my left hand are still wedged between the pages of my book, my stocking cap dangling from my right hand. I drop the cap so I can bury my fingers in his thick hair, which is as soft and silky as his kiss.

When my fingers tighten, a growl sounds deep in his throat. It's the hottest noise I've ever heard, almost as hot as the way his big hands slide down to grip my ass through the thick sweater and lift me higher against the wall. Without hesitation he pushes into the cradle of my thighs. My inner muscles clench with aching need when the hardness of his cock wedges against the soft melting heat of my pussy.

Too many clothes separate us. Desperately, I rock my hips against his, needing that thickness to fill me, needing his entire body to fuck me like his mouth is fucking me.

Except his mouth's not doing that anymore. Abruptly he breaks the kiss and buries his face in my neck, his chest heaving against mine.

Oh god no. He can't stop. In the grip of frenzied arousal, I grind against his heavy erection. "Please."

His tortured groan rumbles against my throat. Strong fingers tighten on my hips to halt my frantic motions.

My next breath is a shuddering plea. "Logan, *please.*"

His big body presses closer, trapping me against the wall, forcing me to stop moving by the sheer weight of his length against mine.

His mouth opens against my throat, leaving a soft hot kiss against my skin before he lifts his head.

"Not Logan," is his gruff reminder. "I'm your Secret Santa. And there's nothing I want more than to finish this, baby. But when I fuck you, it won't be part of an exchange."

My breath catches. "When you do?"

"Yeah. *When.*" Slowly he sets me down, my back sliding against the wall and my pussy dragging over the long length of his erection before my feet hit the floor. "So you tell me, Emma — if I show up tomorrow, there'll be no gifts to put on a balance sheet. I'll just be coming to fuck you. Are you going to open your door?"

I don't hesitate. "Yes."

The swiftness of my reply seems to amuse him. "You don't want to think about it for a minute?"

"No." Though I should. We work together and I desperately need this job. Sleeping with Logan could be the biggest mistake I ever make.

It doesn't feel like a mistake, though. It feels…right.

Or maybe I just *want* it to feel right.

"All right, then." Big hands still gripping my ass through the thick sweater, he gives my butt a squeeze, then lets loose a half laugh, half groan. "You feel so damn good. I better get out of here before my control snaps and I screw you right up against this wall."

"You should anyway," I tempt him with a saucy grin.

This time his response is pure groan. "You're so fucking beautiful. You smile at me and I might do anything. But right now"—his grip tightens on my bottom—"I've got another quick exchange in mind. You figure that mask costs about as much as your panties?"

A naughty little thrill ripples through me. "Maybe about the same."

"You wearing some under this sweater?"

"Yes." It's a breathless reply. "And my pajama shorts."

"I don't want you freezing under there, so I'll just be taking your panties. Are they your favorites?"

I shake my head.

"Good thing. Because after all the unholy things I'll be doing to them tonight, you probably won't want them back."

I'd rather he did those unholy things to *me*.

Though this might be close enough. With the mask covering my eyes, I can't see him sink in front of me. I don't know if he's crouching or on his knees. I just know that his shoulders are somewhere on level with my waist, because my arms looped around his neck are much lower now.

Then I lose even that contact, when he grips my wrists and brings my arms back to my sides. Pausing for a moment, he angles the book I'm still holding, as if to read the cover, then says softly, "Is this what you were doing in here before I showed up—you were curled up under that blanket on your couch, reading?"

"My exciting Saturday night," I say wryly. "Me and a stack of library books."

"Smart is exciting. And it's sexy as hell." Long fingers skim up the back of my calves. "So are these striped stockings. Fuck. I'll spend the rest of my life picturing you wearing these while I've got your feet up on my shoulders and I'm burying my cock inside your sweet pussy as deep as I can get."

Need crashes through me at the onslaught of images those words paint, my inner muscles clenching painfully hard. Softly I whimper, my thighs tensing under his fingers.

A deep chuckle reaches my ears. "You like me saying I'm going to fill up your pussy with my thick cock? You like that dirty talk?"

I guess I do. Cheeks suddenly hot, I nod in response—unable to speak, because my entire body is trembling with tension as his fingers reach the hem of my shorts.

"These first." His voice is rougher now, his big hands reaching beneath my long sweater to grip the elasticized waistband. "Go ahead and step out of them."

The flannel is a soft whisper down my legs. Obediently I lift my right foot, followed by my left.

"Hold onto these." He curls the fingers of my left hand around flannel. "I'm going in again for my prize."

And he's taking the long way up, his palms sliding up the sides of my calves, long fingers brushing the backs of my knees, smoothing over the bare skin of my thighs. Then higher, curving up over my hips, and the cool air inside the room slips beneath the sweater, like an icy breath against the wetness slicking my inner thighs.

"You're shaking, Emma." Callused fingers trace the lacy edge of my waistband. "You all right?"

Dying. But better than I've ever been.

I nod, then clench my teeth against a tortured moan as he begins dragging my panties down my legs. My sweater's too long for him to see anything, but I feel so bare, so exposed.

And so aroused.

His breathing is harsh and slow. "Now step out—"

Abruptly his hands stop, my panties just above my knees.

"They're soaked." His voice is thick and guttural. "Your panties are just fucking soaked."

I knew they were wet but that sounds as if they're far wetter than they should be. My face burning, I awkwardly try to press my thighs together, to trap and hide the offending garment—and freeze when he growls.

"Don't you fucking dare." Roughly he shoves my long sweater up to my waist, then a deep groan rips from his chest. "Your pretty little cunt's dripping with your sweet juices, baby. God help me. I tried. I was going to leave without taking more. But I can't leave you like this."

Scorching heat suddenly engulfs my pussy. My breath explodes from my lungs, my body stiffening with shock.

Logan's mouth.

That's Logan's *mouth*.

And his tongue, roughly stroking my clit. I cry out, my book dropping from nerveless fingers, my knees almost folding—but Logan's strong hands pin my hips against the wall. His ravenous growl reverberates over my sensitive flesh, and this is what I thought his kiss would be, but that was tender and sweet and slow, and this is ravaging, devouring. His hard fingers drag my panties the rest of the way down my legs, then he grips my left thigh and hooks my knee over his shoulder, opening me wider to the fierce hunger of his mouth.

Breath coming in sobbing little pants, I fist my fingers in his hair, and I can't stop the mindless rocking of my pussy against his face. The ruthless assault of his lips and tongue has completely shattered my control—if I ever had any.

With Logan, I don't think I do. There's just need and pleasure like I *never* imagined.

He lifts away from me just long enough to murmur harshly, "You taste so fucking good, Emma. So sweet and hot. I'll never get enough of this pussy."

My pussy won't ever get enough of *him*. My hips buck uncontrollably against his grip, desire spiraling tighter and tighter with every devastating lick, each one hotter, wetter.

Back arching, I cry out again when his firm lips close around my clit and he begins sucking on that sensitive bud, tongue flicking relentlessly. An orgasm approaches, but it's nothing like the ones I've given myself with my fingers before, that sweet shaking release that ends with a soft pulse through my inner flesh and a contented sigh. This bears down on me like a freight train, hard and fast and unstoppable. A ragged scream rips from my throat when it hits, my entire body clenching as convulsions rhythmically squeeze my inner muscles.

"Fuck, yes." Logan backs off my painfully sensitive clit, groaning hungrily as his broad tongue glides up the length of my slit. "Give me all your sweet cum, baby."

My body still shaking with aftershocks, I collapse back against the wall, moaning softly as Logan slowly licks through the saturated folds of my pussy, his tongue dipping past my untouched entrance as if he won't be satisfied until he's lapped up every creamy drop.

Except his mouth only makes me wet again. And if he intends to continue licking, then I have no intention of stopping him.

Though maybe I should have. Because he works me right up to the edge before suddenly slipping my knee off his shoulder and rising to his feet.

A deep chuckle against my mouth is followed by a light kiss. "That'll keep you going until tomorrow."

Oh my god. He's going to leave me like this? "You're an evil Santa."

"An evil Santa with a big dick." He kisses me again, then lifts his head with a soft reluctant groan. "A dick that'll be aching all damn night. I'm going now while I can. You keep that mask on until I shut that door behind me. You all right?"

Never better. "Yes."

"Tomorrow, then." His mouth covers mine again, hard

and possessive, and while I'm reeling from the erotic taste of my arousal on his tongue, he pulls away.

I'm still panting against the wall when the door snaps shut. Heart racing, I push the mask up and stare at the tree across the room. There's a cardboard box on the floor beside it—I didn't realize he carried that in, too. Colorful, unwrapped packages are piled inside.

Christmas lights, I realize. Ornaments.

Logan knew I didn't have a tree. So he must have guessed I wouldn't have decorations, either. Tears burn my eyes, and I stand there for a long minute with a thick knot in my throat, wondering how my life changed so suddenly and so completely with one knock at my door. I don't know what to expect now.

Except I can expect a fucking tomorrow. I'm all in for that. Which might be stupid and reckless, but it feels so right and I want it *so* much—and I rarely treat myself to anything I want.

And maybe a fucking is *all* that I'm in for. Something unexpected and hot and wonderful.

Then done.

I ignore the pain that thought brings as I step back into my flannel shorts. My tree needs decorating. And maybe I won't have Logan forever. But I apparently have him wanting me for a little while—and that's one gift I won't haggle over. Until this ends, I'll take each day as it comes.

Even if the only day I get is tomorrow.

FOUR
Logan

"ONE MORE STOP," MY DAD says, crossing an address off our list and tossing the clipboard onto the dash of my truck. "Then you can go take care of whatever's been eating at you."

It's Emma. She's been eating at me.

Emma and her freezing apartment.

Driving around today with my dad, delivering meals and gifts to low income families, we've been to plenty of places where the thermostat is kept low, where parents and kids are bundled up inside their own homes. So I know what Emma's doing, and I'd love to take care of that electric bill for her. I'd love to take care of anything she needs.

But taking care of her *is* the problem. I've got a real

bad feeling that throwing my money at her troubles will push her away. Just as she started pulling away on Friday, when I said I'd treat her to a drink. I want to be there for her in a way that she won't put on a goddamn balance sheet.

I just don't know what that is yet.

So frustration's been tearing at me since I left her last night. It's ripping at me now as I start up the truck, because her freezing apartment isn't my only worry.

I think I fucked up.

Last night I left her with the impression that the only reason I was coming back was for sex — thinking I'd keep it simple, so I could ease her into a deeper relationship over time.

But I don't think I can settle for just fucking, even for a short time. I want more *now*.

And I want to take care of her, give her everything I can. It killed me to drive away last night, leaving her in that cold apartment. Even knowing she was bundled up and safe — and that it probably wasn't her first night spent huddled under a blanket.

But it will be her last, damn it. "Who's next?"

"Millie Atwater."

He doesn't need to give me her address. Millie Atwater's been our last stop the past twelve years, ever since her granddaughter and her granddaughter's boyfriend got put away for selling meth, and Millie took in two young great-grandchildren.

Not so young anymore. Teenagers now, both of them.

Probably at an age when receiving gifts and a holiday meal through a families-in-need program is more embarrassing than exciting, but when we arrived the weekend before Thanksgiving, I didn't see anything other than welcome on their faces. And as Millie's getting on in years, now they take care of their great-grandmother as much as she took care of them.

"You worried about that job in Florida this week?" my dad asks.

For a custom installation. Some bigwig ordered a bed too big to fit through any entrance, so I'll be flying across the country and assembling the parts we've already shipped to the site. Which I've done before, plenty of times—I figure if they're paying us six figures for a bed, then the least I can do is put it together at the location of their choice.

I won't like being away for three days while I'm starting up this relationship with Emma, but the installation itself isn't a problem. "No. That's all set," I tell him.

"You worried about Lucy being alone?"

Lucy, the stray dog that's adopted my house as her own. "No. Patrick will be stopping by to check in on her."

"Is it Emma?"

I shoot a surprised glance at my dad, trying to read his face. Beneath the Santa hat he's wearing, his expression's as neutral as it's ever been, which tells me he deliberately looks that way. My dad's not neutral about anything.

But there's no point in denying it. If he's got a problem

with me chasing after his new office manager, it's better to hash it out now.

"Yeah, it's Emma," I tell him.

Slowly he nods, and I see the glimmer of worry I expected to see before. But I don't expect his reply.

"You be careful with her, son," he says solemnly.

My back goes up. "What the hell does that mean?"

My dad knows me. He knows I'm not going to fuck around with an employee, not unless I'm dead serious about her.

And I am.

"It just means that she hasn't always had it easy."

I know that. I'm surprised he does. "Are you talking about her foster homes—did she tell you something about them?"

"She didn't have to. I saw it for myself."

I frown at him. "When?"

"Six, maybe seven years back, when we were out delivering boxes. It was a house over on south Washington. One of the Christmas runs, it must have been, because you were right behind me with a box of wrapped gifts."

"*I* met her before?"

And don't remember? That can't be right. Seeing her for the first time a few weeks ago was like a kick in the balls and like coming home to a warm holiday meal, all at once. Six or seven years ago, she'd have been fifteen or sixteen, so she probably looked about the same as she does now. I can't imagine my reaction to her being much different when I was twenty.

"You didn't meet her. Probably didn't even see her. Because I was ahead of you when she opened the door. A little skinnier than she is now, and I'll never forget those big eyes, or the way she lit up when she saw my Santa hat. Or the way she *really* lit up when she saw the box I was carrying."

Which would have been a frozen turkey and all the dinner fixings, if I'd been carrying the wrapped gifts.

And I'm starting to remember this. "That was the time you called up Linda."

A friend of his who works in Child Services. It was one of the few times in my life I've seen him pissed. He'd been terrifyingly quiet as we headed back to the truck, and we sat there for a full ten minutes, while he watched that house as if debating whether to storm back in. Finally he used his cell to call his friend, and didn't tell me to drive away until after she reassured him that the girl would be taken care of that same day.

What had his conversation with Linda been about? Some bruises that he'd seen?

Dread settles in my gut like lead. "What happened?"

"She was wearing a long sleeved shirt, but the sleeves were rolled up—doing dishes, I think. And there were marks all over her wrists and just above. I didn't know what to make of them until her foster mother shows up at the door smelling like a whiskey factory. She grabs the girl by arm—hard enough you could tell it was hurting her—and the woman yanks her back into the house, hissing at me that they didn't need any charity. Then she slammed the door in my face."

Not the first door we've had slammed in our faces. Probably won't be the last. But it was the first time my dad ever called up Child Services after.

Rage has a burning lock on my throat, but I manage to ask, "Did Linda follow up with you?"

"I didn't give her a chance. I called her up the next day. She had one of their social workers visit that afternoon and had the girl in another house by that evening." His gaze slides over to meet mine. "It was the girl's sixth placement that year, Linda told me. Said some kids are difficult to place, they've got issues or special needs, but this was nothing the girl had done. Just shitty luck and a string of crappy homes that had slipped through the cracks. But when I followed up again a few weeks later, the girl seemed to have settled in all right to her new home. 'The girl,'" he suddenly says again, then chuckles. "Didn't know her name was Emma until she showed up for that interview."

"Did she recognize you?"

He shakes his head. "Back then, I don't think she really saw anything except the Santa hat and the box I was carrying. And don't you ever tell her."

"I won't." Emma might not care that my dad witnessed what had happened, or she might feel embarrassed and ashamed—or worry that it had something to do with being hired. She wouldn't have any reason to worry, but pride isn't always a rational thing. I wouldn't risk hurting her. "Does Marianne know?"

"No." And apparently my dad's thinking the same thing because he adds, "It was her references and interview that got her hired. Not pity."

I never questioned that. So I just nod, waiting for him to continue.

"Anyway," my dad says. "That girl has stayed with me all these years. Because I'll never forget how she looked at that box—like I was bringing her everything she ever hoped for. And I'll never forget the way she looked when that door was closing, and she realized she wasn't going to get it." His throat works for a second. "Sometimes she looks at you that way—like she looked at that box. And that's why I'm telling you to be careful with her. Don't give her something, then take it away. And before you start anything, you need to be sure."

"I'm sure," I tell him gruffly. "I'm more certain than I've ever been of anything."

A misty smile touches his eyes, his mouth. "Just like your mother. Always knowing when something's right."

Yeah. And when it's *not* right.

I fucked up last night. Instead of coming to Emma with everything I had to give, I only offered part of it.

That's not what'll happen tonight.

* * *

THIS TIME I DON'T LEAVE a gift box. Just a note.

Put on your mask.

Unlock your door and wait.

Signed,

YOUR SECRET SANTA

I could do this without the mask—but it's sexy as hell on her. I think it excites Emma, too. When we fuck for the first time, though, she won't be wearing it. I'll be looking into her warm brown eyes as I sink my thick cock deep inside the lush heaven of her body.

But a blindfold is just right for an abduction.

When I open her door, Emma's up against the wall where she was standing the night before—and my reaction's about the same seeing her, except this time I know how she tastes. I know the heat of her mouth and the sweetness of her pussy. It's all I can do to stop myself from lifting her against that wall and plunging deep.

I hear the breath she draws as I step inside her living room. I see the lift of her small breasts beneath her pale blue top.

She was expecting me tonight. I think she's done her hair, though I can't really tell, because it always looks so soft and wavy, like I spent all night fucking her, my fingers buried in those thick golden strands. Makeup, too. Though her eyes are covered, her lips are a deep, glossy cherry that makes the color of the red satin mask look cheap in comparison.

Gone are the gloves and the thick sweater that she

was swimming in yesterday. Instead she's wearing one of those little button-up sweaters that give thousands of horny teenagers wet dreams about their school librarian. She's paired it with that swingy little skirt I remember from her first day at work, though this time she isn't wearing tights. She's got striped socks on again. Red and white this time.

There's not a single doubt that I'll be going down on my knees again tonight.

But not yet.

I stride across the room toward the tree. She's decorated the branches and it looks damn pretty, but I'm not leaving the lights on to burn her place down. I yank the cord from the outlet and my gaze sweeps into the tiny kitchen. Nothing on the stove. Her keys are hanging from a peg by the front door.

That's all I need to know.

I head back to Emma, who's pressed up tight against the wall, and her toes are curling nervously against the threadbare carpet while I walk around her living room. Then as soon as I come near, she stops that nervous fidgeting and rises up on those toes, as if seeking a kiss.

Hell. I'm not disappointing her.

I bend my head and claim those cherry lips, loving the hitch of her breath when my tongue sweeps into the hot cavern of her mouth, loving her soft moan as she leans in against my chest and her tension immediately seems to melt. As if she's been waiting for this all day.

So have I. Which is why it's so damn hard to tear my mouth from hers, to stop this cold.

Need roughens my voice as I tell her, "You ready for me to take you, baby?"

A breath shudders through her parted lips, the glossy red smeared a little now and looking sexy as hell. "Yes."

All right, then. In a swift movement, I grip her waist and hoist her up onto my shoulder, her cute ass pointing up and her beautiful head hanging down.

A surprised scream is followed by a roll of her throaty laughter. "Logan!"

"Santa." To punctuate the reminder, I give her butt a little swat. "And like any good Santa, I'm hauling my gift sack around over my shoulder."

"This gift sack can walk into the bedroom, Santa."

If that was where we were going, I'd still carry her in. I stop by the couch long enough to grab the blanket she has folded neatly over one arm, and drape it over Emma's back. That ought to keep her warm until I get her into the truck and get the heaters going again.

Being covered up clues her in to the fact that I might not be taking her to the bed. "Logan?" she asks again, this time with a real question in her voice.

I snatch the keys off the hook and open her door. "Like I said," I tell her as I lock the handle and swing it closed, "I'm taking you."

"Where?"

"My place."

"Why?"

I'll tell her. But not while she's hanging upside down over my shoulder. "So I can show you my Christmas tree."

"Your Christmas tree?" Her giggles shake her against me. "Does your 'Christmas tree' have shiny balls hanging from it?"

Naughty girl. With a laugh, I swat her butt again, then can't stop myself from caressing those sweet curves through the blanket. She's got the sexiest ass.

"There are balls involved," I tell her. "But they're not too shiny."

"Is it a *big* tree?"

"The biggest you've ever seen, baby."

"That's probably true," is her dry response.

I don't want to think about any others she's seen. Jealousy's not something I'm accustomed to—and it's not as if I've been celibate all my life.

Because I didn't know Emma Williams was going to come crashing into it.

I open the truck and gently set her on the passenger seat. Her face is flushed, her mask still on—though it's slipped up above her eyebrows. Her soft brown eyes meet mine for a long moment, and her gaze searches my face, as if she's trying to figure out what I really intend.

Then deliberately, she pulls the mask down to cover her eyes. A smile curves her lips.

That's an invitation to continue if I ever saw one. Quickly I buckle her in and head around the front of the truck.

"Do I smell pizza?" she says the moment I get into the driver's seat.

"Yup." Because eating at someone's house is different from going out to dinner or drinks. No bill arrives at the end of a visit, and she won't feel any obligation to repay me, except maybe to invite me into her place sometime for coffee. "You like pepperoni?"

"Who doesn't?"

Good question. "I figure you'll need your strength after you climb my Christmas tree," I tell her, and her husky laugh goes straight to my cock.

And I can't fucking help myself. With a groan, I reach across the seat and capture her face in my hands, drawing her in for a long taste of her mouth. When I finally let her go, she's breathing hard and her pussy's most likely soaking, which means I don't waste another second before putting the truck in gear and swinging toward home.

"How long until we're there?"

Her voice is strained, her fingers fisted in her lap. She's squirming in her seat like she was during the drive to the bank on Friday. Was she that hot and wet then? Hot and wet and I didn't touch her, didn't taste her?

I won't make the same mistake tonight.

"Ten minutes." Which might end up being the longest of my life. "You gonna make it?"

Her head falls back against the headrest and she gives a tortured laugh. "With or without shoving my fingers beneath my skirt?"

Already stiff and aching, my cock hardens to steel in a sudden, painful rush. "Do it, baby. Let me see you get those fingers all wet. Let me see you make yourself come."

Although then it'll become a real question whether we'll make it to my place without me pulling over and fucking her in my truck.

Biting her lip, she shakes her head. "It's not as good. I want your fingers."

"You'll get them." The promise is low and harsh. "As soon as we get there. My fingers, my tongue. I'll eat you all up, make sure your pussy's all soft and wet before I fuck you deep and hard."

"Oh god." A soft moan escapes her and her back arches, her hips pressing against the taut seatbelt. "Hurry," she pleads, and another frustrated moan is accompanied by a roll of her hips. "Or distract me. Tell me what you did today."

Thought about kissing her, licking her, fucking her. But that's not the distraction she's looking for. Or the one I need if I'm going to get us there in one piece.

"I drove around with my dad. Then spent a few hours at Murphy's watching the game with Shawn and Tyrone." Because I went to Emma's place after finishing up at Millie Atwater's earlier, and she wasn't home. "You?"

"I went to the senior center on Oak."

I glance over. She's pulled her right foot up to the edge of the seat and has wrapped her arms around her knee, as if keeping a tight hold on herself. "You got family there?"

Although, shit—that can't be right. She doesn't know who her parents are.

But she doesn't seem to care that I just shoved my boot into my mouth again. Easily she says, "I was balancing checkbooks."

I grin. "Just grabbing old ladies' checkbooks and balancing them? You really do like those numbers to add up."

With a laugh, she shakes her head. "It's part of that citywide 'donate your professional time to people in need' program. Ever since I worked at the bank, I've been putting in about ten hours at the senior center every month." She rests her cheek on top of her bent knee, her face turned toward me as if looking at me through the mask. "Most of them are on fixed incomes. So sometimes it's just to make sure they don't overdraw or get slammed with fees. Other times because they're more likely to be taken advantage of, so it's to help them keep an eye on what money's being spent. Especially this time of year."

I know that program. My dad and I donate time every month, too. That's what we were doing today. In the winters, that means donating money for gifts and meals, then driving around and delivering them. The rest of the year, we're usually donating labor and materials. Weatherizing houses or repairing leaky roofs, mostly.

"So that was my day," she adds with a dismissive shrug, as if suddenly uncomfortable talking about herself. "How close are we now?"

Not close enough. The distraction's taken a bit of the

edge off. But only a bit. And knowing that we're getting closer and that she's over there needing me as much as I need her just amps it right back up again.

That need's thick in the air between us the rest of the drive. The heavy tension smothers any pretense that we'll be able to distract ourselves from this. Everything's focused on getting her into my house, then getting into her.

Her breathing quickens as I slow to make the turn into my driveway. "Are we here?"

My answer's hardly more than an affirmative grunt. And any other time I'd have her take off that mask, show her my house, because it's part of what I'll be offering her. But I'll have to settle for showing her the inside and letting her see the rest tomorrow morning.

I don't wait for the garage to open. Braking hard in front of my porch, I tell her, "You stay there," before rounding the truck and yanking her door open. A second later I've scooped her up out of her seat and I'm hauling ass up the front steps, carrying her against my chest.

She's giggling again. "You forgot the pizza."

The pizza doesn't need to be fucked. "I'll get it after."

Though I've got to slow this down or I'll be inside her too fast. Our first time ought to be long and sweet, not a quick bang against my front door. So it's better to tease her and get her ready for my cock while that mask is still on. Because I want to be looking into her eyes when I make her mine—and as soon as the mask comes off, as soon as I see her gazing up at me with those big brown eyes, I don't know if I'll have any control.

Kicking my front door closed behind me, I head across the foyer and take the stairs two at a time. Emma's arms tighten around my shoulders, the hem of her skirt fluttering against my hand, her soft lips nibbling along the line of my jaw.

My cock's already about to explode. Christ, I've never needed anyone as much as I need her. But I've got to slow this down.

When I start up the second flight, a little laugh shakes through her. "This is a lot of stairs."

It's a lot of house. My bedroom is on the third floor, a big open loft overlooking the great room. I hit the lights as I reach the top of the stairs, because although she's wearing that mask, I want to see everything.

Starting with how she looks when I lay her on my bed, her golden hair pillowed beneath her head, her lush lips parted and her cheeks flushed. Groaning, I brace my hands beside her shoulders and allow myself a deep kiss before backing up to strip off my coat.

I yank off my boots and look up to see Emma sitting upright, her slender fingers unfastening the last button on her sweater, the sides falling open to reveal the silky white camisole that's clinging to the soft swell of her breasts, her pouting nipples clearly outlined through the thin fabric.

With a hungry growl, I catch her hands and push her flat against the bed again, my fingers trapping her wrists over her head. "Not so fast, baby. No unwrapping the presents until you've sat on Santa's lap and told him what you want."

Plaintively she moans and wriggles her sexy little body beneath me. "I want you inside me, hard and fast."

Ah, Christ. The way she's moving, that camisole's pulling even tighter across her breasts. Beneath the silk, her nipples look as hard as rivets. Those sweet buds must be aching.

Fuck, and I need a taste. Gruffly I ask, "You want me to suck on those pretty tits first?"

Her body goes utterly still except for the shuddering of her breath. "Yes," she whispers.

Holding her wrists in my left hand, I glide my right hand up the smooth length of her bare thigh. She starts to tremble as my palm travels beneath the hem of her skirt. "You want me to tease your clit while I do? You want me to fuck you with my fingers, get you hot and wet enough to take my big cock?"

Accompanied by a desperate moan, her hips lift off the bed as if to urge my slowly drifting hand even closer to its destination.

That's not an answer. Roughly I say, "Tell Santa that you want my fingers fucking your greedy little pussy."

"Yes." She's panting, the muscles of her thighs quivering. "*Yes.*"

My hand travels higher and I almost lose my fucking mind. She's already slippery wet and feverishly hot and there's not a single barrier to my touch. Hanging onto control by a thin thread, I grind out through clenched teeth, "Now tell Santa why you're not wearing any goddamn panties."

"Because—" She cries out as my fingers slick through the sultry lips of her pussy, her hips bucking, her back arching.

"Because?"

Helplessly she rocks her juicy cunt against my palm. "I thought you'd take me against the wall. At my house."

My mouth hovering above hers, I tease her snug entrance with my longest finger. "And you didn't want anything coming between us."

She's utterly still again. "Yes."

"Didn't want anything to slow me down."

"Yes."

My thumb slides up to circle her swollen clit, the blunt tip of my middle finger pressing against her tight little opening. "And you wanted me inside you hard and fast."

"Yes." It's barely a breath.

And I'm going to give her what she wants.

My finger plunges deep at the same moment I capture those cherry red lips, craving the silken heat of her mouth. Her thighs snap closed around my wrist, as if trying to keep me in, but I'm not going anywhere. Her pussy is so unbelievably tight, clamping down on my finger in a scorching vise. I groan against her mouth, already imagining that velvet sheath gripping my thick cock, then lick past her lips, seeking the slick heaven of her kiss.

Instead I find her teeth clenched. Against me, her body's motionless, but it's not the stillness of anticipation. She's tense and shaking, her muscles locked.

As if she's hurting.

Heart thundering painfully in my chest, I lift my head. "Emma?"

She makes a little sound, a whimper through her clenched teeth. Above the manacle of my fingers, her hands are balled into fists, fingernails digging into the heels of her palms.

"Talk to me, baby."

"It's okay. I'm okay." Her ragged voice doesn't sound okay. "I just need another second to adjust."

Another second to adjust…to my *finger*? Oh sweet Christ.

Emma's a virgin. And I just rammed into her with the tenderness of a jackhammer.

Fucking hell. My middle finger's still buried inside her but when I gently try to pull away, her thighs tighten around my wrist. I could overpower her, but I'd have to force her legs apart…and I'm not going to hurt her more than she already is.

Letting go of her wrists, I tug the mask up over her forehead. Her eyes are squeezed shut, tears glittering at the base of her dark lashes.

The sight fucking destroys me. My beautiful fighter. There's a storm of emotions ripping through me, sheer disbelief and primitive satisfaction and soul-sucking guilt—along with gut-wrenching relief that when I got to her apartment, I didn't just slam my cock into her and fuck her against the wall—but at the forefront of everything is the overwhelming need to take care of her now, to erase those tears.

Softly, I kiss the corner of her trembling mouth. "There's no rush, baby. We'll take as long as you need."

"Okay." A teardrop slides down her temple and soaks into her hair. "Sorry."

"No need for sorry."

"Well, *I'm* sorry." She laughs now, a choked little sound. "Because it was going really well."

"It still is going well." To reassure her that we're not finished here, I bend to kiss the side of her throat, where her pulse is racing just beneath her skin. "We'll just slow it way down. Until you adjust. Is it still hurting?"

"Not as much." Her thighs flex against my wrist, subtly pushing my hand against her, as if tentatively testing the feel of my finger moving within her tender flesh. She stops on a sharp breath, but her eyes are open now, the tears gone. That warm brown gaze meets mine and a wry, tremulous smile curves her lips. "I didn't think it would hurt. I've used my own fingers. And…tampons."

Her cheeks go scarlet at the last. Chuckling, I shake my head and hold up my free hand, because showing is more effective than telling. I'm pretty sure my smallest finger is bigger than any tampon. And when I press my palm against hers, the difference in our sizes couldn't be any plainer. She could wear my hand as a baseball mitt.

"Oh," she says softly.

"Oh," I echo teasingly before threading my fingers through hers and pushing her hand over her head again. "So a little change in plan. I'm not fucking you tonight."

Disappointment crumples her expression and boosts my ego about a thousand points. "We still can."

"We can still fool around," I tell her. "But I'm not fucking you until I can get two or three fingers into your pussy without hurting you. We'll take it slow, all right? Bit by bit. Just like a Christmas gift. Sometimes you tear off the wrapping paper, and sometimes you open it real carefully."

Her teeth clench in frustration, and she tilts her hips up, forcing the penetration of my finger a little deeper. "It's not really hurting now."

And her pussy's slowly softening around me. But that doesn't change anything. "That's just one finger. My dick's a lot bigger. And if you're going to be screaming under me, I want it to be because it feels so damn good. Not because my cock is ripping you in half."

"Oh my god." She abruptly stops pushing against my hand. Her face scrunches into an expression of squirming discomfort. "When you put it like that…"

Laughing, I kiss the adorable wrinkles across the bridge of her nose. "I'll still make you feel good, sweetheart. We'll get your pussy used to taking something of this size. Tomorrow I'll give you a little more. And by Christmas I'll be fucking you, all right?"

For a long second, she appears torn between anticipation and disappointment. Finally she sighs. "All right."

Good. And now it's time to ease that disappointment.

The lush heat of her cunt still surrounds my finger. My thumb is nestled in the moist curls above her clit. But as incredible as she feels, I don't move that hand at all as I lean in and claim her cherry red lips. No light and sweet kiss this time. My tongue strokes hers, hot and slick, slowly fucking her mouth until she's moaning low in her throat and her pussy juices are flooding my palm.

When I lift my head her brown eyes are glazed and her lids heavy, as if in a passion-drugged haze. She hasn't eased up with her thighs yet, keeping my wrist trapped and my hand right where it is. The clasp of her virgin pussy is still tight as hell, but her inner walls are softer now, more elastic as her arousal deepens. I watch her expression for any sign of pain when my thumb slides over her swollen clitoris.

Back arching, her hips rock sharply, pushing my finger deeper. Her soft moan is cut off by a strangled cry of pleasure. Frantically rolls her hips as if seeking that same touch.

"Again," she pleads breathlessly. "Do that again."

Fuck, yes. Circling her clit, I gently pump my hand within the taut grip of her thighs. She's so damn wet, her nectar lubricating every thrust, and the sound of my finger fucking her tight channel is slick and sexy and driving me out of my head.

It's driving Emma out of hers, too. She's flushed and writhing, panting on one breath and moaning the next.

No pain left. So it's time for me to unwrap a little bit of my present.

Without slowing the thrust of my hand or the tease of my thumb over her clit, I bend my head and latch onto her left nipple, sucking the hardened flesh through the thin silk of her camisole. She cries out, her wrists tugging against my grip, and I let her go because I need that hand to get some of the clothes out of the way.

They aren't coming off. Not with my right hand caught between her thighs and Emma lying on her back. Wrestling with her sweater isn't on my list of priorities right now, and pushing her camisole higher gives me what I want—more of Emma's beautiful body bared to my gaze.

And she's simply stunning. The white camisole rucked up by her collarbones doesn't look half as silky as her golden skin. Her small tits are soft round mouthfuls, her pouting nipples like rubies at their tips. Her stomach's soft with just a bit of inward curve at her sides that flares into the wider curve of her hips. The high waistline of her flirty skirt conceals her navel, but the hem is flipped up and I've got a full view of her long, long legs and those striped socks. Her knees are bent, her heels digging into the mattress as she rocks her hips to the rhythmic thrust of my finger, trying to take me even deeper.

My big hand's shielding her pussy, but I got an up-close view of that last night—the dark blond curls, the delicate pink flesh nestled between her glistening labia. I got a long, deep taste of all the sweet juices flowing from her virgin well.

But I get to taste the rest of her now.

With a hungry growl, I lower my head to her breast again. Her nipple's hard and hot against my tongue. The moment I suckle that taut bud into my mouth, her pussy clenches around my finger, her moan thick and deep in her throat. Her hands slide into my hair, and I fucking love how wild she is, pulling at me and then pushing as if she's so lost to pleasure she doesn't know what to do with herself, to do with me, and she's just grabbing whatever she can. Circling my tongue around her ruby nipple, I groan against her soft tit as her inner muscles ripple around me again. She's so damn sensitive. The way her cunt squeezes and pulls at my finger, when my big cock's deep inside her it'll be a miracle if I last more than a few seconds.

I won't last much longer *now*. Thrusting into her sultry pussy, tasting her golden skin, hearing her frantic moans, my cock's a throbbing volcanic rock and I'm about to blow a load into my fucking jeans.

But she's close, too. Her fingernails dig into my scalp and my name is a sobbing chant on her lips. There's no rhythm to her movements now, just chaotic need and desperate urgency. Every sound she makes drives me closer to the edge, and there's barely any control left as I move over her, straddling her thighs with my knees digging into the bed, my mouth finding hers again. I fuck my tongue past her lips the same way my finger's fucking into her, the way my cock needs to be fucking into her. Her swollen clit's so slippery with her juices that my thumb's gliding right over with almost no friction, faster and faster, then all at once she arches beneath me, screaming into my mouth as her virgin pussy clamps down, those tight inner muscles strangling my finger, her thighs squeezing my wrist.

And I can't stand it any longer. As soon as she comes down, her thighs falling gently open, I rise up on my knees again. My right hand glistening with her cum, my left hand shaking with need, I tear open my jeans.

Her blond hair tangled around her head, Emma watches me drag my straining cock free of my briefs, her eyes glazed and her lush lips parted. My gaze locks on her flushed face as I fist my aching shaft. Pre-cum is already dripping from the bulging tip, and it only takes three rough strokes before I'm grunting like a fucking animal and cum spurts from my cock in thick streams, splattering across her belly and tits.

Holy fuck. Chest heaving, I collapse over her, barely catching my weight on my elbow. I bury my face in the sweat-slicked skin at her throat, my lungs bellowing like a steam engine.

I can feel the aftershocks passing through her body in erratic shudders. Her arms slip around my shoulders, her fingers threading into the hair on the back of my head, and as incredible as that orgasm felt, it doesn't come close to the feeling of being held by her after.

But I just made a sticky mess all over her chest. And this isn't taking care of her.

With a groan, I summon the strength to rise to my knees again, then can't get any farther because my brain shuts down at the sight of her lying there, her brown eyes glazed with satisfaction and her mouth bare of her cherry lipstick now, but still red and swollen from my kisses. The longer I stare the more she begins looking real shy, biting her lip and lowering her lashes, but she has no reason to worry.

"You're so fucking gorgeous, baby." That hair, those lips, those tits — and my seed painting her skin, splashed across her ruby nipples. But I know damn well how semen itches as it dries, so I tell her, "Don't move. I'll get something to clean you up. You lie right there so my cum doesn't get all over your clothes."

Not just my cum. Faint crimson streaks paint her inner thighs and my hand. Christ. No wonder it hurt her so bad. Not just tight and unaccustomed to taking anything inside her. After twenty-two years, whatever remained of her hymen must have been strong as steel and clinging to her pussy for dear life, and I ripped right through it.

Maybe it's better this way than with my cock, though. We'll take it slow, give her time to heal up.

A warm washcloth in hand, I return to the bed and

find she hasn't moved much — except to tilt her head, looking back across the open floor of the loft, where a tall Douglas fir is decked out in lights and ornaments beneath the peaked roof.

She shoots me a sparkling grin that makes my heart inflate ten sizes larger within my chest. "You really did have a Christmas tree to show me."

Yeah, I did. I lean in for a kiss, then murmur against her smiling lips, "And is it big enough for you?"

Giggling, she wraps her arms around my neck. "Apparently *too* big, considering that it's rip-me-in-half big."

"Then now is probably not the time to tell you that I've got two."

And even better than Emma Williams holding me on my bed after we come our brains out is Emma Williams holding me on my bed and laughing her beautiful head off.

When her laughter begins to taper off, I go in for another kiss. "Now let me clean you up, and then I'll show you my *really* big tree."

And pray that showing her everything else I've got to give her doesn't end up scaring her away.

FIVE

Logan

EMMA DOESN'T HAVE TO GO downstairs before getting a look at my big tree. She can see it from the loft, a fifteen-foot Douglas fir that sits in front of the big windows facing the creek, but it's not until we're in the great room and I plug in the lights that the full height of it hits her. Her mouth drops open and she shakes her head.

"Why one so big?"

That's ripe for another joke, but I hold off this time and give her the truth. "The year I moved in, I had a smaller one in here — and it irritated the shit out me."

Her brows shoot up. "Irritated you?"

I gesture toward the high ceiling, the tall windows. "The proportions were all off. So every time I looked at it was like scraping steel wool over my dick."

"Ohhhhh," she says slowly, her gaze slipping over my face as if seeing something new in me. "It's an artist thing."

I don't know about that. To my mind, I'm a builder, not an artist. But maybe it's the same thing in some ways. Cabinets and furniture are all about proportions, too.

And the irritation when those proportions are out of whack is probably something she understands. "Probably like when you can't find that error throwing a checkbook register off by a few pennies."

There's a flash of acknowledgment in her eyes, then her lips purse and she says dryly, "Yeah, but that doesn't feel like scraping steel wool over my dick."

I grin, and all at once her expression changes, lips parting softly and brown eyes widening as she stares at me.

That's a good expression, I think. A happy expression. But I'm not sure what to make of it. Gruffly I ask, "What?"

A hint of pink touches her cheeks, and her gaze flicks away like it used to when I thought she was scared of me. But this time her eyes come right back to mine again. "You haven't smiled at me before."

That can't be right. "The hell I haven't."

"It's true."

"You sure?"

She nods, then her blush deepens. "At least not that I've seen."

Because maybe every time I grinned at her, she was wearing that mask.

"I like it," she adds now, quietly.

"Well, you've given me a lot of reasons to smile." I catch her cheeks in my hands. "So you'll see it often."

"And your angry face."

"That's not my angry face," I say, but the sudden gleam in her eyes tells me she knows that. It's probably the face she saw as I was stroking my cock and splashing her tits with my cum. "But, yeah. You'll be seeing a lot of that, too."

She grins and I kiss that laughing smile before releasing her.

"Now look around the house if you like. I'm heading out for that pizza."

But she doesn't stray far from the tree in the short time I'm gone. She's standing by the window, looking out over the snow-filled backyard that slopes down toward the woods and the creek, then follows me into the kitchen.

I turn on the oven and slide the pizza inside to reheat. "You want a beer? Wine? Or if you want something harder, I can mix it up."

She slides onto one of the stools tucked up beneath the bar separating the kitchen and the great room. "I'll take a glass of wine."

"Any preferences?" Being a beer man, I don't drink it much myself, but I keep a few bottles on hand for visitors.

"Nothing too sweet." Her gaze alights on the tray at the end of the bar, which holds the collection of carvings I've been working on in my spare time. "Are those more ornaments—like the ones on your tree?"

"Yeah."

"You carved these?" She reaches for the tray, then stops. "Can I — ?"

"Go ahead."

Her slender fingers pick out a tiny crib. "You made all of those carved ornaments on the tree, too?"

"I did. Keeps my hands busy while I'm doing other things." Like waiting for pizza to heat, or watching a game. "But those are for Marianne — for the Secret Santa thing."

A miniature nursery set that matches the full-sized one I'm giving her.

Emma cocks her brow and gives me a look. "So you're her Secret Santa, too?"

I laugh and shake my head. "Not the same. Whose name did you get?"

"It's supposed to be secret. So I'm not telling." Studiously she returns her attention to the other carvings in the tray, as if completely dismissing my presence.

Or trying not to give anything away. Because I saw all the names remaining in the hat after she got hers, and there's a fifty-fifty chance that she picked out my name. Either mine or Shawn's. And the way she's deliberately not looking at me, I'm thinking it isn't Shawn.

But I'll be patient. After fetching her a glass, I screw the cork out of a bottle of chardonnay and pour.

As I'm setting the wine in front of her, she says, "I should probably warn you that I'm a lightweight."

Wordlessly, I take the glass back and tip in more.

She's giggling when I put the wine in front of her

again. Her giggles quiet when she takes a sip, and her expression turns pensive. Her thoughtful gaze remains on me as I pop the cap from my beer, as I take a swig. All the while I return that look, wondering what's going on in her head.

I don't have to wonder for long.

With a sigh, she sets down her wine. "What is this, really?"

"What's what?"

"What are we doing here? This Secret Santa thing. And *this*." She gestures from me to herself. "You could have fucked me at my apartment."

I could have. But that's not all I'm after. And I figure the only way to tell her is bluntly.

"You want to know what this is?" I set my beer down and grip the edge of the counter, my gaze steady on hers as I say, "This time next year, I want you sitting there with my ring on your finger."

Her lips part on a sharp breath. Stunned, her gaze searches my face, and the naked yearning I've seen before in those warm brown eyes has returned.

Then disbelief replaces the longing. "Okay, what is it really?"

"That is 'really.'"

A laugh breaks from her, but it's an uncomfortable laugh, as if she can't figure out what the joke is but she's certain there must be one.

Shit. I didn't expect her to joyfully leap up and start

planning our wedding. I *did* expect the disbelief, but time will prove the truth of what I'm saying.

That discomfort, though — it's as if I've prodded something tender and painful inside her, and hurting her was never my intention.

"It's no joke," I say softly.

The sad yearning filling her eyes again just rips me apart. As if she wants to believe that I'm serious…but simply can't.

So I'll just have to convince her.

With a heavy sigh, she shakes her head. "You don't even know me, Logan."

So her objection isn't *her* not knowing *me*? As if she could picture herself wanting me that much. She's just not picturing me wanting her. "I know enough to be certain you're the one for me."

"How?"

"I just know it. The same way I knew that I was meant to build. The same way I know that room needs a big tree." With a tilt of my head, I indicate the tray of carvings. "Or the same way I can look at a hunk of wood and see what it'll be."

There's a brittle edge to her smile. "So you're going to whittle me down? Cut parts of me away until I'm what you want?"

"Shit, no. So that's a bad analogy. I'm talking about being able to imagine how it'll be between us." And my mouth's running faster than my head, trying to tell something that needs to be shown. I pick up my beer. "Bring your wine and come with me."

After a brief hesitation, she slides off her stool and cups her palm around her glass. Holding out my free hand, I tangle my fingers through hers and start across the great room.

"I designed this house," I tell her as we're passing the stairs, which marks the end of the open floor plan that encompasses the great room and the kitchen. Beyond the stairs is a more traditional layout with enclosed rooms. "It's got everything I want or could imagine wanting in a house. But half the rooms are empty. The bedrooms on the second floor, I figure eventually I'd have a wife, kids—a family to fill up those rooms. And then there's rooms like this."

I watch her face as I swing open the door. No need to look in—I designed the place, I know what's there.

"I installed the shelves myself," I say as her breath catches and her fingers tighten on mine. "Because I wanted a big fucking library, with shelves on every wall. But the thing is, the only books I have are gifts that I've received, because everything I want to read, I download to my phone. So I've got this big empty room. But it never bothered me, because a part of me knew this room was never for me, anyway."

Her gaze flies to mine before she looks away, and there's that yearning again as she takes in all the empty shelves.

"But you can see this room being yours, can't you?" My

voice deepens. "I think you can. You read a lot, so I think you're good at imagining what you can't see. You put on that mask and I bet you're still picturing everything that's happening."

Her cheeks flush and she darts another glance at me. This time I'm the one to look away, but it's so that she'll follow my gaze.

Raising our linked hands, I point to the bay window. "I think you can see yourself curled up there in the summer. And for the winters, I think you can picture a big comfy chair over there by the fireplace, because I sure as hell can imagine me coming in to find you reading on one—and thinking you're so damn sexy that I'm going to fuck you right there."

A shuddering little breath escapes her. Yeah, she's imagining that, too.

Her gaze slides around the library again, and she takes a deep gulp of her wine before abruptly looking to me.

"Oh my god," she says. "You're *Beauty and the Beast*-ing me."

I don't understand any of that. "I'm what?"

"From the Disney movie. You're romancing me with a library."

I take a swallow of my beer and consider that. Finally I nod. "I suppose I am. And I like that you're the kind of girl who can be romanced by a library. But I'll tempt you with anything I have, if I need to."

Her gaze searches mine again. "But I don't understand

what's tempting *you*."

Well, that's easy enough to explain.

"You mean, aside from you being a fighter who's still standing after all you've been through in your life? Aside from how you can be independent and say a balance sheet is less complicated than relationships, but still be so friendly and open at the same time? Aside from how sweet your mouth and your pussy taste? Aside from how you don't want to owe anybody anything, but you'll donate your time without any expectation of receiving something in return?" My fingers tightening on hers, I tug her closer. "Or maybe it's just because I'm about to take that pizza out of the oven and head to the couch, and I think you'll come with me. And I don't imagine either one of us will be doing anything much different from what we usually do on Sunday evenings, but somehow it'll be a hell of a lot better than it usually is, simply because we're here doing it together."

"That last part sounds really nice." Her eyes are soft and shining, her voice thick. "So what will we be doing on that couch?"

"Watching a movie, maybe." It doesn't matter, as long as she's with me. "Have you seen the one based on that Martian book you were reading yesterday?"

"Not yet."

"Then that's what we'll do." Because although I haven't erased her doubts, she's not running away—and when I bend my head, she rises to meet my kiss. Good enough for now.

Back in the kitchen, I'm not surprised to find my mutt standing in front of the oven. Emma's eyes widen and a pretty smile lights up her face.

"Who's this?"

"Lucy," I say, nudging the dog out of the way so I can open the oven door.

"Can I pet her?"

"Sure."

Setting her wine aside, Emma sinks onto her heels and starts scratching behind Lucy's ears. I don't stop her because this is another time when showing is better than telling.

Lucy looks up at Emma, who's telling her what a pretty girl she is, before walking away in the middle of the petting as if the human doesn't even exist.

"She's more like a cat than a dog," I say, sliding the pizza back into the cardboard box. "One day she showed up at my door, so I started feeding her. Now she's got a doggie door and a blanket on the far end of my couch, but I might as well be a nail in the wall for all the interest she shows in me. Whenever there's food available, she's right there, but otherwise she doesn't have any time for our human bullshit. Will you grab me another beer? Might as well bring that bottle of wine, too. You want a plate or are you all set with a napkin?"

"Napkin's good," she says and follows me to the big sectional sofa facing the flat screen. "Did you design all your own furniture, too?"

"This couch? Nah." I drop the pizza box onto the coffee table. "Some of the stuff in the house is out of the Crenshaw catalog, but this couch is from IKEA."

She chokes on her wine.

Grinning, I take the extra bottles out of her hand and set them next to the pizza box. "The way I see it, if I'm going to be spending time making furniture, I might as well make the company some money while I'm at it. That won't happen if I'm only building pieces to furnish my own house."

"Practical," she says, eyeing the couch as if trying to decide where she's supposed to sit.

"Yeah, it is." So are all the pockets for the remote and the cupholders that the IKEA shit comes with. "Why don't you take the chaise. I'll park my ass on the cushion next to it and put my feet up on the table here."

Gingerly she sits and scoots back against the cushy arm, legs curled up and those striped socks folded beneath her. Since she's not using the long end of the chaise, I move the pizza box there, where it'll be within easier reach for both of us.

And this is the fucking life. A sexy girl on my sofa, her wine in one hand and a pizza slice in the other. I've got my beer, a remote, and I couldn't ask for a damn thing more. I pull up the movie rentals onscreen.

As I'm flipping through the categories, Emma says, "I thought you watched football on Sundays?"

"Usually. But I'd rather do this with you." Though honesty forces me to add, "You won't be offended if I check the scores on my phone while we're watching, will you?"

"I won't be offended. But you should just put on football, instead."

I glance at her. She's got a bite of pizza between her teeth and is fighting with a long string of melted cheese that won't let go of her slice. "You like football?"

Mouth full, her initial answer is a shrug, then she finally wins the war with the cheese and swallows her bite before she tells me, "I like the exciting parts."

"The exciting parts?"

"Yep." She picks off a pepperoni and pops it into her mouth. "When you start yelling at the TV, that's my cue to start watching."

Chuckling, I reach past her for my second slice. "Sounds like you've done that before."

"I've lived with my share of families who had sports fans. And it was always the same—I'd be reading, and look up when someone started yelling, and I'd get to see the best parts of the game without having to slog through the boring parts."

"So you plan to read while I watch the game?"

"Unless you'd feel ignored."

"With you snuggled up against me? Hell no."

"All right. Although since your library shelves are practically empty, you'll have to let me use your phone." Her eyes take on a mischievous gleam. "You have books downloaded, right? I bet I can find something to read in there."

Hopefully. I hand over the device and ask, "I'm about to be judged, aren't I?"

She grins at me. "Oh yes."

And she really does start scrolling through all the titles as soon as she opens up the app. Holy shit. Never in my life would I have thought a woman looking through my digital library might be a nerve-wracking experience, but I never knew that woman would be Emma Williams. I try to see all the books through her eyes. I'm not a real highbrow reader. I've got some histories and biographies, but most of what I read are mysteries, thrillers, and horror off the bestseller lists. Anything with action and that doesn't spend too much time navel-gazing.

Now I'm spending more time watching her face than watching the game. She's sipping her wine while she continues scrolling through — as if looking at all the books I have is just as entertaining to her as reading them.

Suddenly I can't take the suspense anymore. Gruffly I ask her, "Have I lost all hope?"

"I'd say the opposite. In fact, you're in real danger of me stealing your phone," she says mildly, without looking up from the screen. "This is one of the mystery books that Rowling wrote under her other name, isn't it?"

I glance at the cover. "I think so. I don't pay much attention to the authors themselves. Just whether I like what they're writing."

"Did you like this one?"

"Yeah, it was all right. Don't start with that one, though—start with the first book. It's in there."

"Okay."

A few moments later she opens the first book and settles in, and my heart's suddenly ten times bigger than it was last Sunday when I was sitting here, wondering how and when I'd get Emma Williams to stop being afraid of me.

My dick feels ten times bigger, too. But I ignore it as best I can. Emma's likely still hurting from earlier, and although I plan to get my mouth on her later, my cock's going to have to wait a bit longer.

Until halftime rolls around, and Emma leans forward to set her wineglass on the table—then slips off the sofa and kneels on the floor between my legs. She looks up at me with heavy-lidded eyes, and the instant rush of blood to my cock has me gritting my teeth and struggling for control even before she's touched me.

"It's all right?" she asks softly, placing her hands on my knees.

"Fuck yes," I groan the response from low in my throat. Then I make myself tell her, "You don't have to."

"I know. But I want to." She starts running those hands up the tense muscles of my thighs and I'm in heaven. "But will you do something for me?"

"Any fucking thing in the world."

The ferocity of that response pulls a smile from her. "I

just want you to take off your shirt. So I can look while I— Oh."

I'm already dragging it over my head and tossing it onto the table before leaning back against the cushion again. Her soft lips part, her gaze slipping over my torso. I'm never going to be one of those male model types, all waxed and lean. I'm built solidly, with thick muscles and a hairy chest.

The way Emma's looking at me, that's just fine with her. Her breathing gets heavier, her gaze dropping as her hands reach the V of my thighs. She hesitates, then skips right over the bulge of my erection, heading straight for my belt buckle.

And I realize what I should have realized the moment her knees hit the floor. "You ever done this before?"

"No." Her wry gaze flicks up to mine before returning my waist, where she's pulling my belt free. She opens the snap and starts easing the zipper down. "But I've seen some porn. Plus I've read a lot of books. And I…"

Her voice trails off. With the pressure of denim and the zipper easing up, my cock's already trying to bust free. I drag the elastic waist of my briefs down over the base of my shaft, and maybe she didn't get a good look before when I was stroking myself, but she sure does now. Thick and long, the fat head an angry red and already beaded with pre-cum.

"Oh," she whispers.

"You changing your mind?"

"No. It's just… I've imagined this. And, um. You're bigger."

And getting harder with her every word. But although it's killing me, I'm going to let her take her sweet time.

"What else did you imagine?"

Nervously she licks her lips, gaze darting to my face. "You looking like you do now. But I thought you were angry."

So I was mean and had her on her knees. "And what'd you do?"

Her eyes locked on mine, she leans forward until her hot breath is torturing the head of my cock. Her voice is a throaty whisper as she says, "Then you told me to make you come."

My dick's never been so fucking hard. On a low growl I tell her, "Make me come, then."

She moans as if that harsh demand is the sexiest thing she's ever heard. But the sexiest thing is her small hand wrapping around my thick shaft. It's her mouth opening up over the head of my cock. It's her pink tongue darting out to taste the drop of pre-cum at the tip.

Fuuuuck. My breath hisses through my teeth. I fist my hands in the cushions, stopping myself from burying my fingers in her hair and shoving my cock to the back of her throat and commanding her to suck.

It's her first time. It becomes a chant in my head, a mantra to keep control. *Her first time. Go easy.*

But Emma doesn't go easy on me. She bends over

my cock, wraps both hands around my meaty shaft, and takes as much as she can into the sultry torment of her mouth. Without prompting, she starts sucking on me. Sucking and working her tongue and letting all that drool lubricate the twisting stroke of her hands, like she knows exactly what she's doing, but her inexperience is there in the careful way she never takes me deep enough to risk choking, as if she thinks gagging on my cock might ruin the effect instead of making it all even hotter. But that careful attention, that innocence is so fucking sexy. I can't look away, can't stop groaning her name. Her golden hair's a wavy curtain framing the erotic perfection of her face, those full lips wrapped around my dick — and her hungry gaze keeps flicking up to meet mine as if checking to see if she's doing this right, but it couldn't be any righter. She could be all teeth and jelly fingers and I'd still be ready to come just from that hungry look in her eyes telling me how much she wants this, how much she wants me to love it.

And I love it too damn much. My control's slipping with every slick caress of her tongue, every wet pull of her mouth, every tight pump of her hands.

"Harder now, baby." Through clenched teeth I make the rough demand. "You feel so goddamn good, sucking my dick like that. A little harder and you're gonna make me come."

As if just the thought of me coming deepens her own arousal, she moans around my cock. Immediately her rhythm becomes faster, harder.

"Fuck." Groaning, I fist my hands deeper into the cushions. Only a miracle is stopping me from thrusting into her mouth, from fucking her face. *Her first time.* But that thought isn't working as a leash on my control anymore. Because Emma Williams is sucking a cock for the very first time and it's mine.

The only cock she's ever wanted is *mine*.

"Gonna come, baby," I grit out. My big hands wrap around hers, tightening our grip on my shaft. "Pull back unless you want my cum filling up your mouth."

Oh fuck, she *does* want it. Because she doesn't pull back. Instead she makes a deep hungry sound and sucks harder, and that's the fucking end of me. The orgasm bulldozes into me, my cock jerking in her grip and my cum exploding past her lips. Too deep, because now she chokes a little and draws back until just the bulging crown is in her mouth, but I couldn't stop this now if I wanted to, and her face, sweet Jesus. Her face — her eyes locked on mine and her skin flushed and her full lips still sucking right at the tip. Another pulse shoots down the length of my shaft as that look wrings every drop of cum from my dick.

Holy shit. My chest heaving too hard to get a word out, I cup her cheeks. It takes her a long second before she swallows my cum and she makes a funny face as she does it, and the next second I'm laughing breathlessly when she reaches for her wine and chases the taste by draining her glass.

"You'll get used to it," I tell her and she laughs, cheeks bright red and eyes gleaming. Then she laughs again when I add, "You must read some dirty, dirty books if that's where you learned to suck cock like that."

"Some." Smiling, she crawls up onto my lap, straddling my thighs as she kisses me with the flavor of chardonnay and cum on her lips. It's sexy as hell, and so is knowing that she's got no panties under her skirt, and her bare pussy is hovering right above my bare dick.

It's enough to get my cock stirring again and my mouth watering. "Are you wet?"

"Mmm-hmm," she hums against my lips, then says, "But halftime's over."

"Fuck the game."

She giggles and kisses me again. "And just think of how hot I'll be if I have to wait—sitting next to you, knowing that as soon as the game's done, you intend to eat my pussy. With every play, I'll be thinking about how much closer I am to having your mouth on me. Think of how wet I'll be *then*."

I'm not sure who she's trying to get hotter, me or her—but it's working.

"All right," I tell her, and she looks damn satisfied as she scoots over. After I tuck away my cock, I open my second beer and refill her wine, then sit back again.

This time when she starts reading, she turns sideways, leaning back against the cushioned arm of the sofa and draping her long legs over my lap. The hem of her skirt slides up, just a little. Not enough to see anything beneath. But these next two quarters are going to fucking kill me.

I slide my palm up one of those long striped socks before letting my hand rest on her lower thigh, my fingers stroking the inside of her knee.

This is the fucking life, I decide — a beer, a game, and a hot pussy waiting for me.

But I'm wrong. Because about five minutes later, I look over, and Emma's not reading anymore. Instead her eyes are closed and my phone is lying on her chest with her hand still loosely clasped around it. Beneath her sweater, her small breasts rise and fall on deep, even breaths.

And *this* is the life. The best life. One that's even better than I imagined. One where Emma is comfortable enough and trusts me enough that she'll fall asleep right next to me. Now I just have to persuade her that a life together would be better than she can imagine, too.

Starting with when she wakes up.

SIX

Emma

THE GAME MUST BE OVER.

I didn't intend to nap, but I can't think of a better way to wake up than with Logan's tongue dragging over my clit. Oh my god. My pussy's already wet and aching, as if he's been trying to nudge me out of sleep for a while, and my body's way ahead of my brain.

Softly I moan, reaching for him. My fingers tangle in his hair as he lifts his head. He must have spread me out on the chaise, because I'm lying flat with my thighs open wide, and my feet aren't dangling off the cushions. Everything's dark—not due to the mask, because I'm faintly aware of Christmas lights shining somewhere off to the side—but as if he's already turned off the television and all the lamps.

Voice low and rough with amusement, he says, "Finally awake, then?"

Not all the way but getting there. "Mmm."

He seems to take that as a signal to redouble his efforts. His mouth lowers again, the firm grip of his hands pushing my thighs wider. Hungrily he latches onto my clit and even as I'm crying out with the agonizing pleasure of it, his fingers slip through my slick folds and press against my entrance.

"Let me know if it hurts, baby," he says gruffly, then begins easing a finger inside of me.

It doesn't hurt. The initial penetration stings a little, but then his tongue glides over my clit, and it just feels wondrous and full.

"It's good," I pant breathlessly. "So good."

A low groan is his response, his mouth never leaving my clit, his hand slowly thrusting. And I must have been close to an orgasm before I woke up, because I'm *so* close now, almost frantic with the need to come—then stiffening, stiffening, as a sharp stretching ache builds at the entrance of my sex. Because he's added another finger. Slowly he pushes it deeper, watching me, and it hurts but the pain's already fading, until I'm just left with that feeling of being stretched and overfilled.

"All right?"

"Yes," I whisper, though I'm not really too sure—until his mouth lowers again, and he slowly licks and tugs at my clit, and his fingers start thrusting gently, deeper and deeper. Then I'm truly all right, beyond all right, the sensations racing through me becoming more acute with every lick, every pump of his hand. And suddenly I'm right there again, right on the edge, but I'm higher, dizzy with the sheer pleasure of his touch. Then the world narrows with sudden solid clarity, narrows to the width of my skin and the stroke of his tongue, the incredible fullness of his fingers. I come with my back bowing, choking on my scream, my pussy squeezing that wonderful thickness inside me.

Groaning, Logan rides out my orgasm, then gently withdraws his fingers and softly licks the cream from my pussy lips before rising over me. His mouth finds mine in the dark, the tang of my arousal on his tongue and lips, and he smells so good—like soap and some woodsy fragrance.

Too soon, he breaks the kiss and murmurs against my lips, "Good morning."

"Good morning," I reply before I even realize what I've said. Then I do, and a couple of things hit me all at once.

It's Monday morning.

Logan is showered and fully dressed.

And I'm in his bed.

My gaze shoots to the window. Still dark out. But that doesn't mean anything. This time of year, the sun doesn't come up until *after* I'm supposed to be at work. "Oh my god. What time is it?"

"Six thirty." With a grin, he stands and reaches for my hand to pull me up with him. "If you want to hop in the shower, I'll head down and start the coffee and some breakfast."

Six thirty. No need to panic, then. Except I feel panicky, anyway.

I try to hide it, smiling and babbling something like, "Shower, good, okay," before rushing to the bathroom. Inside, I stare at my flushed face in the mirror. My heart's racing and anxiety knots my gut. Because last night was perfect. *So* perfect. This morning was, too. But now reality's going to set in.

And I don't want it to.

But it does. It always does. That's when those amazing things he said last night — about us being together, about putting a ring on my finger — he won't be so certain about those things anymore. There will be something, *something* that changes his mind. And he won't want me any longer.

At least he wants me now. For a little while.

With two shower heads featuring multiple massage settings, beautiful cream tile and glass doors, his shower's as oversized and as incredible as the rest of his house is. I want to linger but I rush through, and emerge smelling as good as Logan did earlier. The anxiety in my gut has loosened some, but a heavy ache has taken up residence in my chest. Because I *can* see myself here, in this house, in this bedroom. I can see myself with Logan.

And when this is over, everything I imagine having

with him is going to haunt me for the rest of my life.

I find a sweatshirt and sweatpants waiting for me, laid out on the bed. They're both far too big, but I'm able to pull the drawstring on the waist of the pants tight enough that they don't slide down over my hips. My own clothes I fold into a little pile and carry down the stairs with me.

The scent of coffee and bacon leads me to the kitchen. The rumble of my stomach sounds louder than my footsteps, and seems to announce my presence.

In a blue flannel shirt and black Carhartt carpenter pants, Logan looks up from the pan of scrambled eggs that he's scooping onto a pair of plates. Appreciation lights his icy blue eyes when he sees me in his sweats, but he doesn't say a word. He just lets his eyes tell me that he'd eat me up again, even when I'm drowning in shapeless clothes.

My cheeks heat. Feeling suddenly shy, I head for the coffee. "Did you already pour yourself one?"

"Yeah." He sets a mug and two plates on the bar. "You need cream and sugar?"

I shake my head. He takes the stool at the end of the bar—where he'll be sitting adjacent to me, instead of sitting side by side. We'll be looking at each other, I realize. And there will be no hiding from him.

I wonder if he knows I *want* to hide.

I set my mug next to my plate—then realize I might have been wrong about our seating arrangement. "This isn't mine, is it?"

It's piled high with more eggs and bacon than I can possibly eat. But a glance at the other plate tells me that it's just as full.

"Too much?" He takes the other stool. "I just made double of what I usually make."

Laughing, I demonstrate the same thing he demonstrated to me last night—holding up my hand against his. "That size difference is probably a good guideline for meal proportions, too."

"I guess I'm just not used to cooking for a woman," he says casually, as if he has no idea how telling me that lifts through my chest like some sweet song. "Eat what you can and we'll give Lucy the rest. And maybe she'll like us a bit better afterward."

I glance over to where the yellow dog is curled up on the floor in front of the refrigerator door, her eyes locked on Logan's big hands. "You think she might?"

"Nah. I've given her hundreds of these." He picks up a crispy piece of bacon from his plate and Lucy lifts her head. "And she wouldn't care if I got hit by a truck tomorrow, as long as the people who moved in here after my funeral still fed her."

He tosses the bacon Lucy's way. She leaps up and scarfs it out of the air, then lies down again—with her back to us, as if to let us know that she still doesn't care about our existence.

I grin and take a piece, too, but I'm not throwing it to the dog. Instead I start in on my own breakfast.

Logan digs in, too, and he's quiet until he's about halfway through. Then he says, "What are you doing on Christmas Day? Are you going to your friend Traci's place?"

Mouth full, I shake my head.

He frowns. "Are you staying at home by yourself?"

"Yes." It's what I've done every year since leaving my last foster home.

"Come with me to my dad's house." His pale blue gaze is steady on my face. "Spend it with us. It's just him and me."

Sharp yearning tightens my chest. But I shake my head. "Thank you, though."

"Why no?" He asks it softly.

I poke at my eggs. "It's just hard…being the outsider during Christmas."

"You speaking from experience?"

"Yes." And because I can see he's not going to just let this go without an explanation, I sigh and set down my fork. "I had some great foster families. And all of them had either their own kids, or relatives who showed up during the holidays. Whenever they did, they'd tell me, 'You must be so grateful to be a part of this great family.' And I *was* grateful, but…I never really felt a part."

"Of the family?"

"Yes." I don't think I can force down any more food through my aching throat, so I wrap my hands around my coffee mug, taking comfort in the warmth. "I was just there, looking in at what they had. But *I* never had it."

His jaw is tight. "Especially not when they said shit like that—telling you how you're lucky to be included."

I nod. "So Christmas was when I was never allowed to forget that any happiness I felt was due to someone else's generosity, and how I owe them for that."

His gaze is intense on mine, his voice like gravel. "It's not true generosity if they expect something in return—even if all they expect is gratitude. You don't owe anyone a damn thing, Emma."

"Well…some things I do." I owe a lot to those families. "I guess I just don't like it thrown in my face."

"Name one person who does," he says dryly, and the smile that reply pulls from me makes it easier to swallow when I take my next sip of coffee. "What about the families that weren't great? Did they do that, too?"

"Yes, but it wasn't exactly the same. I wouldn't have wanted to be a part of their families. And most of the time, they made it clear that anything I got would never have been given anyway, except as part of their obligation as a foster parent."

"Those gifts are the ones that came with a price?"

"Yes. Nothing was ever freely given. It was always held over our heads. One misstep, and either we wouldn't get it—or it would be taken away. Or they'd use it to remind us of what we owed them."

"If you came to my dad's, everything would be freely given. I have a feeling it would be at Traci's, too."

"I know it would be." And I do. Just like everything

that Logan's given me here has been. "But I don't want to be the outsider."

"Well, that's a simple fix." A smile tilts the corners of his firm mouth but the solemn gravity of his gaze doesn't lighten. "We'll make you part of our family."

Sheer longing grips my heart. Oh my god, and he said it so *easily*. Eyes stinging, I try to cover my reaction by taking another sip of steaming coffee.

Gaze narrowing on my face, he leans in. "That's the solution, right? You won't be on the outside looking in if you become a part of a family—or if you make a new one. My dad and me, we'll be yours. And we'll keep you around Crenshaw's for a long, long time."

Though my throat's aching and thick, I manage a tiny smile. "That does sound really nice."

Eyes piercing, he regards me for endless moment. "But you don't really trust it, do you?"

I shrug.

"Why?" When I don't answer, he says gruffly, "You say I don't know you, baby. But I want to."

And there's no reason not to tell him. It's all ancient history. *Kind of* ancient history, since it still affects me now. But maybe while he needs the explanation, I need the reminder—because when Logan says he'll make me a part of his family, I want it so much.

But I've wanted it before.

I pull in a shuddering breath. "When I was little, there were a couple of times I thought I might become part of a family. Permanently a part of one.”

“Adopted?”

“Yes. By the time I was older, I didn’t expect it anymore. Younger kids are more likely to be adopted—and of course when I was little, I didn’t know about the statistics, but the foster parents I was with would say certain things that made me think it was a possibility, and I’d hope. But there was always some deal breaker.”

His eyebrows draw together in a dark frown. “What do you mean—a deal breaker? Their application was rejected?”

“No.” That word sounds hoarse, so I take another sip before continuing. “It was always something about me. I didn’t look enough like them, so no one would ever believe I was their real kid. Or I wasn’t interested in the right hobbies or sports, and they wanted a kid who liked the things they did.”

Those icy eyes suddenly burn with anger, and he’s staring at me with his jaw clenched. “They *told* you this?”

“Not directly.” I shrug. “But I don’t think adults realize how much kids overhear. Or how much they pick up. There was one woman, I remember. I was five, and she used to take me to those beauty pageants for little girls. We were getting ready backstage, and she’s brushing my hair while she’s talking to one of the other moms—and the other woman asked her if she would make it permanent, because I was so pretty. And my foster mom said, ‘My husband and I were thinking about it, but she doesn’t really have any stage talent.'" And after all these years, I can still hear that response so clearly. After all these years, it still tastes so bitter. "Because I couldn't sing, or play an instrument, or dance. And she didn't think adding numbers in my head was a real talent. So that was the deal breaker. There was just always *something*."

Logan reaches across the bar and folds my hands in his. "So you're thinking I'm going to find something I don't like about you, and it'll be a deal breaker for me."

God. And he just zeroed right in on everything that's hurting my heart. Zeroed right in, and threw it out there in the open. Tears burning in my eyes, I try to pull away, but his fingers only tighten around mine.

"I won't," he says fiercely. "I won't, Emma."

I shake my head. The inside of my chest feels scraped raw. "You don't know me. And when you do—"

"I'll just want you more."

He sounds so sure. And it hurts so much, because I so desperately want to believe him.

But I don't know if I can dare to hope again.

His voice softens. "I'd put that ring on your finger now, Emma. I'd make it permanent right now. But I'm not asking that of you yet. I'm just asking you to share Christmas with us, so you can see how it might be. But you won't have to imagine anything. You'll see it's real—and so good—when it's happening. Just like last night was better than I imagined it would be. So think about coming, okay? There doesn't have to be any gifts involved. We'll just watch football and drink beer and then go for a walk in the snow along the creek, then sit down to dinner and eat more of my dad's Christmas roast than we should. Then I'll take you home and fuck you so hard."

A watery laugh bursts from me. Because of course it would come down to that between us.

His eyes gleam with amusement. "That last part has almost convinced you, hasn't it?"

All of it sounds wonderful. But the last part is just easiest to believe in. I know he wants me sexually. I want him, too. There's nothing to doubt there.

"Just think about coming," he says now, gently. "We'd love to have you with us."

Drawing in a deep breath, I gather my courage. "Okay. I'll think about it."

"Then think about this, too." His big hands cup my cheeks, keeping my gaze locked on his. "No matter what I might give you, you'll never owe me anything. That doesn't mean I won't ever ask anything from you, because I might ask a hell of a lot. When I get that ring on your finger, it means asking for your patience and your trust and your faith and your heart. But even if I ask for all that, you don't *owe* it. You should only do it because you want to give it. Because it makes you happy to give it. And everything I do for you, it'll be because I want to. Because it makes me happy. All right?"

His face is wavering through my tears. "All right," I whisper, and he kisses me, his mouth so warm, his hands so strong.

And my stupid heart begins to hope. But kissing him back makes me happy—and I want it more than anything.

So I do, for as long as I can.

It's not long enough.

Since I wasn't wearing any shoes when he abducted me, Logan has to carry me out to his truck—then into my apartment when we reach it.

As I'm unlocking the door, I tell him, "It'll just take me a couple of minutes to change clothes. Do you mind giving my car a jump before you take off?"

I lead us into the living room, which smells like cold pine—the best smell in the world, truly. But I don't think that I'll associate the scent with Christmas anymore. Instead I'll think of the man who's coming into the apartment right behind me.

"I don't mind giving you a jump, but since I'm flying out first thing tomorrow, I've got a better solution," he says.

"To that job in Florida?" My heart sinks a little. I'd forgotten about it—but he'll be gone for three days.

Right now, that seems like a lifetime. Three days is longer than how much time has passed from the moment he first kissed me to now.

Everything has changed so swiftly in that time…and I'm terrified that in three days, everything will change again.

"Yeah." As if he's just as reluctant to go as I am for him

to be gone, Logan catches my hand and pulls me back for a sweet kiss before lifting his head. "Shawn's picking me up around four in the morning so we can head up to the airport. Why don't you stay with me tonight, then continuing staying at my place and using my truck until I get back on Thursday?"

Using the truck makes a little sense, considering the state of my car's battery. Staying at his house doesn't. "Why?"

"You need a reliable rig. I need someone to look after Lucy."

"Like house sitting?"

"Yeah. Like house sitting."

He says that as if he's just agreeing with me—not as if house sitting was how he was thinking of my stay there until I mentioned it.

Suspiciously I narrow my eyes at him. "You didn't make arrangements for Lucy already? I find that hard to believe."

"Of course I did. Patrick looks in on her, but he can't stay overnight. I'd rather have someone there." His voice deepens and he cups my face in his warm hands. "And I like the thought of you sleeping in my bed, Emma—or reading on my couch. And you can find out a lot about a man by being in his house. While you're there, you could look through anything. I don't care. Search my closets, my drawers. Poke around in my workshop. Dig through my computer. I'll give you all my passwords. I'll leave my tablet so you can read all my books. And I'll call you every night and whisper dirty things in your ear before you go to bed. All right?"

I don't know how I can say no to that, though I should. The more time I spend at his place, the more clearly I'll be able to imagine myself staying forever—and the harder it will be when this is over.

Not that it matters. It will be hard no matter when it ends. Today, tomorrow. Next month. It will always be harder.

So three days of harder is nothing.

"All right," I agree softly.

When he kisses me again, it still makes me as happy as it did before. I still want it more than anything. And it still doesn't last long enough.

I don't think it ever will.

SEVEN

Emma

I T FEELS LIKE MUCH LONGER than three days — and two nights.

Two nights spent warm and cozy in Logan's bed, reading his books, and talking with him over the phone — calls that end with his voice rough in my ear, telling me to come hard for him.

Two nights of coming for him, so hard.

Thursday seems to stretch out even more endlessly than the other two days did. I try to focus on work, hoping that the minutes will fly by more quickly. But the minutes begin dragging by even slower when Shawn calls into the office to let us know that a weather delay and traffic will put their arrival about an hour behind schedule.

Forty-five minutes later, I'm staring morosely at

the clock on my computer when Marianne swings by, as cheery as ever. "Our Christmas party guests will be arriving soon, so go ahead and pack this up, hon—then run in to Bruce's office for a few minutes. Oh, and here's your Christmas bonus."

I stare at the envelope she drops on my desk. "A bonus?"

"Mmm-hmm." A concerned frown suddenly etches a line between her brows, and she leans in, her voice lowering. "You're going to see everyone's bonuses when they clear the account, so when you see the amount, I hope you don't feel as if you are appreciated less than anyone else. It's just that it's your first Christmas with Crenshaw's, so it won't be as much as some of the others."

"Oh, no—I just wasn't expecting a bonus at all." They hadn't been mentioned when Marianne and I ran the payroll this week.

"It's a little something that Bruce always writes up at the end of year. He considers it profit sharing, and he puts aside a percentage of his earnings to split up every Christmas—and the employees who've been here longest get the bigger share. So an employee who's put five years into the company receives five times as much as someone in their first year."

She says that last part with an apologetic tone again—as if still explaining why mine might be smaller. But I don't care how big it is. My throat's a burning lump as I say, "That must be a good incentive to stay."

Marianne gives me a look as if I just said the

understatement of the year. "This is my tenth year—and that bonus is part of the reason it's so hard to leave."

"I can imagine." Thickly I say, "Thank you."

"You thank Bruce." She winks at me. "And it's past five o'clock somewhere in the world, so why don't you take him a little eggnog when you go in."

Nodding, I slide the envelope into my purse. Despite my curiosity, I won't tear it open and look. No matter how much it is, it's more money than I had before. Even if it's only twenty-five dollars, it means I can budget in a little host gift for Bruce when I go with Logan to his dad's house for Christmas.

It doesn't even occur to me until I'm knocking on his office door that I've officially made the decision to go.

Bruce calls for me to come in, then rises out of his chair with a broad smile when he sees the cup I'm holding. "Thank you, Emma. You didn't get one for yourself?"

Remembering how one glass of wine put me to sleep, I shake my head. "Probably better if I don't."

My boss grins, and it looks so much like his son's grin that my heart aches from missing him. "Well, if you decide to indulge, let me know if you need a ride home."

Hopefully I'll be getting a ride from his son. But I simply say, "Thank you. And thank you for the Christmas bonus."

He waves that off. "This company wouldn't be where it is without everyone putting their effort in. So I'm always happy to give something back. Did you pick up your Secret Santa gift off the party table yet?"

"Not yet."

His blue eyes are twinkling. "I think he got you something that you'll really enjoy."

Remembering the note and the mask Logan left at my door, I can't stop my blush. I know that's not what Bruce is referring to, but I can't help thinking that a Secret Santa *did* give me something I really enjoyed.

If Bruce notices my blush, he doesn't comment on it. Instead he gestures to the seating area by the window. Outside it's snowing again, fat flakes slowly drifting down. "Come chat with me for a minute, Emma."

This sounds more serious than I anticipated. Anxiety twists in my stomach as I sit.

He settles in and says, "Logan says you might be joining us at my place for Christmas."

My heart's pounding. "I think I will. If it's all right?"

"You'll always be welcome at my house, Emma. Not just Christmas. Anytime you like." And that's just like his son, too — offering it so easily and so sincerely, it makes my throat tighten and eyes sting. "Now, tell me how you're getting on here. Marianne says you're not having any problems and that we'll be in good hands on Monday when you start going it alone, but I want to hear it from you. Are you enjoying the work?"

"I am." I put all the truth of that in my voice.

"Logan tells me you like numbers but don't like the phones."

Every muscle in my body tenses. "Phones are all right, too."

On a sudden laugh, Bruce rocks forward in his chair. "Look at you. You just jumped to the worst possible conclusion, didn't you? Maybe worrying that you not liking phones will lose you this job."

I'd like to join in his laughter, but I can't. Because he's right. I'm terrified.

"Let me reassure you, then." He sits back again. "After that HGTV show, when we began expanding, I hired Marianne to help with the bookkeeping and the front office, while I took care of the back office here. Our catalog was taking off, Logan was making our custom shop into something special, and so she took the administrative pressure off me, seeing that payroll and bills were taken care of. While back here, I made sure everything was running smoothly in our shops. Because that takes up most of my time—coordinating shipments, managing inventory, all that."

He pauses as if waiting for a response. I'm not sure how this is supposed to reassure me yet, but I'm following along. Nodding, I tell him, "All right."

"Now, there's a reason I hired you specifically, Emma. That construction company you were with—you didn't just do their bookkeeping. When they started shedding their staff, you handled all their purchase orders, coordinated all of their material deliveries, the scheduling. Yeah?"

"Yes."

"And your boss there said that you were damn good at it. That you picked it all up without a hitch. He said that if they'd hired you two or three years earlier, maybe they wouldn't have had so many conflicts and delays that put them in the red and then put them under. So these past three weeks have been a walk in the park for you, haven't they?"

I'm not sure if I should say yes. "It's true that I have fewer responsibilities here."

His eyes are piercing mine. "Do you like that?"

I don't *dis*like it. But I could be more useful to this company than I am now. "I'd be happy to take on more, if that's what you're asking."

"It is." All at once he seems to sit easier, as if a huge weight just dropped from his shoulders. "I started this company with wood in my hands, Emma, but all I've had in my hands the past ten years is paper. And I miss being in the shop. I miss it like hell. So maybe over the next six months or so, I could show you this side of the business, move you into this office—and hire someone else to answer phones."

My chest is suddenly tight. "I'd like that," I tell me.

"Me, too." Expression satisfied, he looks around the office. "You taking over all this would be the best Christmas present anyone could ever give me. Aside from that mug."

He gestures to the *World's #1 Dad* mug that never seems too far out of his reach.

I can't stop my grin. "Did Logan get you that?"

"It was my Secret Santa gift last year. He never admitted that it was from him, but…"

Who else would give him a *World's #1 Dad* mug? "Right."

"He's a thoughtful boy. Knows exactly what someone needs." Bruce raises his brows and gives me a significant look. "Even if they don't know it themselves."

He couldn't possibly know about the satin mask or how Logan pinned my hips to a wall and licked me to a screaming orgasm, but my face goes scarlet anyway. Because I definitely got what I needed.

A sharp knock at the door saves me, drawing Bruce's attention. Before he even replies to the knock, the door swings open and Logan strides through, his pale blue gaze fixed on me, his voice a low growl. "Marianne said you were in here. Christ, I've missed you."

My heart leaps into my throat, my gaze eating him up as he crosses the room with that long unhurried stride—and my ass is rooted to the spot. Bruce is sitting right here. Is Logan going to kiss me in front of him? Because he certainly looks as if he intends to.

Mildly my boss says, "Have I been missed?"

"Good to see you, too, Dad." Gripping the arms of my chair in his big hands, Logan leans down and swiftly touches his lips to mine. Voice low and intimate, he asks me, "How you doing, baby?"

There's apparently no point in hiding anything in front of his dad. Softly I reply, "Better now that you're back."

"Good to hear." His gaze burns into mine. "How's

my dog?"

"Still indifferent to human life."

"And my truck?"

"Also indifferent to human life."

He grins and lightly kisses me again before turning to look at his father. "I think you've got guests in the front office."

Expression amused, Bruce looks to me. "Well, let me make certain we're through here first. I think we've settled everything. Haven't we, Emma?"

Filled with so much happiness that I wouldn't be surprised if someone said it was shining like a rainbow out of my eyes, I nod. "I think so."

"Then you and Logan can discuss what kind of desk you want him to make after you move in here." Eggnog in hand, Bruce rises to his feet. "I think if we rearrange this seating area and stick it over in that corner of the room, she'll have a nice view out the window. Maybe you should take a few minutes and make some measurements, son, before joining the party."

"I'll do that." Eyes slightly narrowed, Logan looks to me as his dad heads for the door. "You're moving in here?"

Quietly I reply, "I think I've been promoted. Your dad says he wants to work in the shop again."

That news seems to make Logan as happy as it made his dad, then the office door clicks shut, and in the next moment my face is in his hands and his mouth claiming my lips in a scorching kiss. My fingers tangle in his hair, and I softly moan when he lifts his head far too early.

"Shit." He pulls me to my feet and kisses me again before stopping, holding my face close, his ragged breaths mingling with mine. "I'll be walking around the party with my dick trying to bust out of my pants if I kiss you much more. So let's go out there, mingle, and leave as soon as we can."

"No arguments here," I tell him.

"If you had any, I'd just throw you over my shoulder and carry you off, anyway. Which reminds me"—he steps back and pulls two envelopes out of his back pocket, one apparently his bonus and the other a red holiday envelope—"I stopped by the conference room when I was looking for you. This had your name on it."

I take the red envelope. "My Secret Santa gift?"

"Yup."

"This isn't a pair of scented candles."

"You don't need those now that you've got a tree." He gives the envelope seal an encouraging tap. "So let's see what he ended up giving you."

I arch a brow at him. "You don't know?"

Grinning, he shakes his head. "Though I gave him a few ideas."

Good ideas, apparently. I carefully break the envelope seal and withdraw a gift card, and my smile is huge when I turn it around to show him. "From that bookstore downtown."

"Just right." He looks as pleased by his dad's choice

as I am, then his gaze narrows on mine. "My gift wasn't on the table yet."

"Your Secret Santa is a slacker." With a laugh, I tuck away the card again, then grip his shirt collar and pull him down for another kiss. Against his lips I say huskily, "But don't worry. You won't end the day disappointed. Maybe I've got a little present for you tonight."

He grins against my mouth. "Oh yeah?"

"Mmm-hmm. A virgin pussy all wrapped up and waiting to go under your big Christmas tree."

Logan's big body tenses against mine. Catching my face in his big hands, he draws back, his pale blue gaze searching my eyes. "I don't want our first time to be like that, baby."

"Not...like what? With a virgin pussy? Because it's not going to get devirginized without you."

"I don't want it to be an exchange."

"An exchange?" I blink up at him in confusion, mentally rewinding our conversation. Slowly I realize where he's going with this, but I still can't quite believe it. "You...think I'm giving you my virginity in lieu of a Secret Santa gift?"

"I don't know," he says hoarsely. "But I know you're strapped for cash. I know you don't like to owe anyone. And that you like to keep things even."

Pain blooms through my chest. "I like *money* to be equal. Sex shouldn't even enter into it."

His jaw tightens, then on a heavy sigh he says, "You kissed me to keep things even when I brought the tree."

The hurt blossoms into anger. Pointedly I stab my finger into his chest. "No," I hiss at him, "*you* kissed *me*. I would have taken the tree as the gift it was. I was uncomfortable with the cost of it, sure. But *you're* the one who suggested that I should make up the difference—and I didn't think it was seriously a monetary repayment. I thought you kissed me because you *wanted* to kiss me."

Logan's face stills and I can see the realization sweep through his gaze. Because it all happened *exactly* as I just said. "I did do that."

Yeah, he did. I lift my chin. "So why do you think I kissed you back? Do you really think it was repayment?"

"No." Eyes closing, he drags his hands through his hair. "No, I don't."

"Good." My throat's raw, my eyes stinging. "Because if I was going repay people that way, I would have let someone at the electric company fuck me. Or I'd bang the guy at the auto shop. But I never thought of whoring myself out." His face whitens and my voice breaks as soon as the word *whoring* leaves my tongue. "It's great to know that you think I would."

"Emma, baby, no." Eyes tormented, his big hand catches mine.

"Don't touch me!" I yank my hand from his grip, stumbling back. "I don't want to touch you. Now that I know you think I'm trading myself for ten dollars instead of giving myself freely. God. If I'd said yes to your ring, would you think I was doing it for your house, your money?"

"No. Emma." His face bleak, he comes after me. "What I said about an exchange, I fucked it all up, because that's not what I meant. I swear to God, it's not."

Maybe he means that. I don't know. I just know that I'm so angry and hurt that I've got to get out of here before I start bawling. Blinded by tears, I haul open the door, hitting a wall of Christmas music and chatter. The party. Oh god. I have to walk through that, holding my head high. Somehow.

Gentle hands circle my waist. "Emma, please."

I hear the pain and apology in his voice, but I don't look back. If I do I'll just cry, and anger is the only thing that's going to get me through this.

So instead of tears, a harsh laugh rips from me, and I say, "You know what the funny thing is? I didn't even pick your name. So I'm going to take my cupcakes back from Shawn and let him pop my cherry instead, since apparently that's what I'm giving up as my Secret Santa gift."

Then I tear out of his embrace and slam the office door behind me.

EIGHT
Logan

MY DAD WARNED ME. CHRIST, he warned me to be careful with her.

But I wasn't — and this time I'm the reason all the sweet hope and joy vanished from her eyes, replaced by hurt and despair. I don't wonder that a girl haunted him all these years. Emma's naked pain and her tears are going to haunt me for the rest of my life.

And if the rest of my life is what it takes, that's how long I'll spend making up for it.

But I don't rush after her. Hurrying is how I fucked up. In my rush to understand her, to know her, I took one thing she told me about herself and applied it across the board, making assumptions I never should have.

Assumptions that I'd have realized were incredibly

fucking stupid, if I'd taken one second to think about them. But I didn't.

So I'm taking a second now. More than a second. Because when I go after her, I can't fuck this up again.

My heart's a heavy lump when I finally leave my dad's office. Immediately I run into Marianne, who's smiling and teary-eyed, the miniature nursery set in her hands.

"This is so wonderful, Logan." She pulls me down to kiss my cheek. "Thank you."

Throat tight, I only nod. My gaze is searching the front office for Emma.

"And here's yours, honey." Stopping by her desk—Emma's desk now—she opens one of the file cabinet drawers and withdraws a wrapped box. She presses the gift into my hands. "I know it's supposed to be secret, but I worried the context would be lost if you didn't know who it was from, and you'd be thinking double-yew-tee-eff when you opened it."

"Thank you," I say in a thick voice.

Her gaze narrows. "You all right, honey?"

"Just looking for Emma."

Her face softens. "Ah, well. She came through here in a rush a few minutes ago. So maybe she's in the restroom?"

She's not. She's not in the kitchen, the conference room, or the reception area, either. I swing back by my dad's office again, just to check, but she's not there.

What the hell?

She didn't drive off. Through the window in my dad's

office I can see my truck. It's still out in the parking lot, covered in snow. She didn't get a ride. No one's left the party yet. She wouldn't walk home through the snow. She's angry and hurt, not foolish.

My gaze narrows on the shop across the lot. Maybe she's there. It would be easy enough for her to grab the keys and hike across the lot.

Still carrying Marianne's gift, I head outside. The Christmas music from inside the office is spilling out over the lot, so it takes me a moment to realize what else I'm hearing.

My truck's engine. A faint trail of exhaust rises from the tailpipe. So she's in there with the heater running, but hasn't bothered to clear the snow from the windows. She's not going anywhere. She's just hiding. And I've got a good idea why.

She doesn't want anyone to see her crying.

My heart aching, I stalk over to the truck and tap my fingers on the driver's side window. A moment later I hear the pop of the locks.

When I open the door, she's all the way across the seat on the passenger side, her face averted and wiping tears from her cheeks. Feeling as if a hacksaw is ripping my chest open, I haul up into the seat and pull the door closed, surrounding us in a cocoon of steel and glass and snow. I set the wrapped gift on the seat beside me. The overhead light goes off.

In the quiet darkness, my voice is a rough mess. "I'm

so sorry, Emma. If I'd stopped to think for a second about what I was implying, I'd have known I was way off base."

"It doesn't matter." Her quavering voice and the tears still spilling down her cheeks immediately prove that's a lie. If it didn't matter, she wouldn't be crying. "Can you drive me home? I'm not going back to the party looking like this."

With a tearstained face that's my fucking fault. But I don't think she wants to hear any more apologies now. I don't think she wants to hear anything from me right now. So I silently grab the scraper and clear off the windows, then remain quiet on the drive to her apartment.

As soon as I stop, she grabs her purse and opens her door, hopping out. "Thanks for the ride."

She slams the door. As if she expects me to drive away.

Or as if she *wants* me to drive away.

That thought hurts like a motherfucker, but it doesn't matter. Whether she's expecting it or wanting it, I'm not leaving. I won't rush her, but I'm not backing off, either.

Emma's already at her apartment door when I catch up to her. Her mascara's in a raccoon mask around her eyes, but some of the angry fire has returned to her gaze. My fighter. I knocked her down but she's up again.

Lips tight, she twists her key in the lock. "You really think you're coming in?"

"You said you had a virgin pussy all wrapped up for me."

"And you said you didn't want it," she snaps back and shoves her door open.

I'm behind her even as she turns to slam it in my face. Instead I have her up against the door a second later, my hand seizing her wrists and holding them over her head as she struggles against me.

Using my weight to trap her against the door, I lower my face to hers and growl, "I want it. I want *everything* you have to give. But I was so damn wrong about it not being an exchange. Every time you give yourself freely to me, Emma, you'll get something in return."

Renewed rage sparks in her eyes. "I don't want anything in return!"

"That's too bad, because you're going to get *me*," I say hoarsely, and her struggles abruptly cease. "You're going to get these rough hands that need to touch you. These eyes that will never tire of looking at you. These arms that will hold you steady or lift you up whenever you need their strength. This head that's crazy about every little thing you do." My voice deepens. "And you're going to get this heart that's already fallen in love with you."

Lips trembling, she looks up at me with wonder filling her big brown eyes. "Logan…"

Releasing her wrists, I gently catch her beautiful face in my hands. "And my big cock. You're going to get that, too."

Her sudden bright smile and husky laugh lift through me, easing the heavy ache in my chest. And I want to kiss her, but I'm not done yet.

"And my big mouth, baby," I add gruffly. "I'm so sorry."

"I know." Her eyes soften, and her hands come up to

stroke my jaw, her touch the sweetest heaven. "I know you didn't mean it." Her breath shudders, and her fingers slip back to link together behind my neck. "But I think I've been waiting for you to find that deal breaker. Me being a whore seemed like it must be."

Ah, Christ. "Honest to God, even if you were, it wouldn't be a deal breaker for me." When she begins to laugh, as if that was supposed to be a joke, I shake my head and meet her gaze with mine. "Listen," I tell her solemnly. "Those supposed deal breakers that made you feel like you were lacking something—those were just excuses those assholes made so they wouldn't have to give anything to someone else. They just wanted to love little clones of themselves. They weren't willing to risk enough, to love someone else enough. But *I* will love you enough, Emma. You could be after my money and I'd love you so much that you wouldn't have any choice but to fall for me anyway."

A tremulous smile curves her lips. "That sounds about right. I don't think any woman has a chance against you."

"Too bad for them. I don't want any woman but you."

Another sigh shudders from her. She cradles my face in her hands. Her voice is soft as she confesses, "I'm in danger of falling so hard and so fast for you."

"Good." It's thick and rough. "Because I've already fallen hard. So I'll be right here waiting to catch you."

She whispers my name, her eyes shining with sudden tears, and her gaze earnestly searches mine. "I want you to know, that just because I'm not moving as fast as you, it doesn't mean I don't want you, or that I can't imagine a future with you. I want that *so* much. I just—"

"Have more reason to be wary."

"Not *more* reason. In the end, we're both risking the same thing. I'm just more accustomed to not getting what I want than you are, I think."

That's probably true. "So you're saying I'm a spoiled asshole."

I expect her to laugh, but instead she shakes her head and says softly, "No. I think you're an example of the universe actually rewarding someone who deserves to be rewarded. You give so much of yourself and so freely."

My heart swells. "Not any more than you do, baby. You're so damn perfect."

Her brows arch. "I have a temper."

Only a bit of one, and I like it when she fires it at me. "It works out. You have a temper, I don't. So we'll balance each other out."

She purses her lips. "I suspect that even if you did have a temper, you'd say that would work out, too."

"I would. Because no matter what, I see it working. If I had a temper, I'd say we'd be in for some sparks flying between us." Tempted by those full lips, I lower my mouth to say against hers, "But we already generate plenty of sparks, yeah?"

"Yes," she breathes. "So can you please fuck me now?"

Hell yes, I can. Mouth capturing hers, I sweep her

sexy little body up against my chest, carrying her into the bedroom. She's already trying to remove her clothes, twisting in my arms while trying not to break the kiss. But her house is still freezing and I'm not undressing her until she's covered.

Even if she's only covered with me.

Her room is simply decorated and neatly kept. There's nothing to trip over on my way to the bed. I toss her into the middle and come down over her, my mouth fucking hers, only raising my head to strip off her shirt and mine. Then I thread my fingers into her long golden hair and bring her back for another kiss.

But I need to taste more of her. Hungrily I capture her ruby nipple between my lips, her skin taut with cold, and she gasps as if burned by the heat of my mouth.

I rise up over her again, dragging one of the blankets with me all the way up to her shoulders before I disappear under it. I hear her laugh, then her sharp breath as my mouth reaches her stomach. Slowly I unbutton her jeans and drag them down her long legs, followed by her panties. The heady scent of her pussy fills the trapped air.

After three days, I'm starving for a taste.

Palming the underside of her thighs with my big hands, I spread her wide. Christ, her cunt's so fucking pretty. Pink and just dripping with juices.

A ravenous groan explodes from me on the first lick. Her flavor bursts over my tongue, salty and sweet, and I can't get enough. Lowering my head, I lose myself in the taste of her. Emma's hands fist in my hair and her erotic cries ring in my ears as I feast, suckling her clit, then dipping past her virgin entrance for more of her silky nectar. She's still so tight, snug around the thrust of my tongue.

Returning to her clit, I slide two fingers deep. She tenses before moaning, her pussy walls slowly accepting the thick intrusion.

My cock's even thicker. So although I'm dying to sink into her and the inside of my jeans is sticky with the precum steadily dripping from the head of my dick, I take my time, lingering over her clit until the first ripples of her orgasm begin tightening her inner muscles. Then I add a third finger and do it again, until she's screaming and her hips are thrashing and we're both dripping with sweat. With shaking hands I shed my jeans and rip open a condom before settling between her thighs.

She's flushed, passion glazing her brown eyes, her lower lip swollen as if she's been biting it between her screams of pleasure. Leisurely I kiss her, my cock full of urgent need but my heart so content.

"Ready, baby?" I ask softly.

Her answer is another kiss, and her long legs circling my hips. Carefully I slide the head of my cock through the slick burning heat of her pussy, lodging against her entrance.

The delicate tissues there don't give way easily. I watch her face as I push harder, feeling the taut stretch around my cock's sensitive crown. Her warm eyes are locked on mine, and she bites her bottom lip again, a whimper sounding low in her throat.

Then her breathless, "Don't stop."

I won't. Threading my fingers through hers, I bear down. She gives a sharp cry, her fingers convulsively squeezing mine, and my teeth clench in sweet agony as the engorged head of my cock is suddenly enveloped in the tight, hot grip of her pussy. I push deeper, until my full length is buried inside her swollen channel, then go utterly still except for the soft kisses I press to her trembling lips.

"All right?" Tension and arousal grind each word to gravel.

Her eyes are gleaming with moisture as she nods, so I wait, slowly kissing her cheeks, her brow, sipping the tears from the corners of her eyes.

Tentatively she rocks her hips, the subtle movement sending a surge of pleasure through my cock.

I watch her face for any sign of pain. "Still all right?"

Breathlessly she nods, then bucks beneath me, driving my cock deeper into her slick pussy, and even as I'm gritting my teeth against the need to slam into her deep and hard, I hear her sharp gasp.

A little pain there. Softly I kiss her again, murmuring, "There's no hurry now, baby. We've got the rest of our lives to fuck hard and fast."

A shaky breath escapes her. "Okay."

Her quavering reply is a greater-pleasure than the mind-blowing sensation of her cunt gripping my cock.

Because that reply is an agreement that we'll be spending the rest of our lives together. A surge of possessive need pours through me in a heady rush, and I lower my head to claim her mouth again.

To claim *her*. Because I've tasted her sweetness. I've taken her innocence.

She's mine now.

Forever.

Bracing my elbows beside her shoulders, I begin moving inside her. Slowly, so slowly, withdrawing the full length of my rock hard erection before pressing back in, the taut inner walls of her virgin sheath reluctantly yielding to thickness of my cock with every deep stroke.

With a ragged moan, Emma breaks the kiss, her hands flattening against my back as if to use that solid plane for leverage. "Faster," she gasps, tilting her hips. "Oh my god. Faster now, Logan."

But I go slow. Even as she scratches at my shoulders, begging frantically for more, harder, please.

Slow. Even as she cries out my name with every endless thrust into the sultry grip of her pussy, her body writhing and her legs wrapping tighter around my hips to urge me deeper, faster.

Slow. Even as her cries become helpless panting sobs, ecstasy riding the edge of frustration that sharpens to erotic agony when I slip my fingers between us to find the swollen bud of her clit.

Slow. Until she bows beneath me, the inner muscles of

her cunt clenching around my cock like a tight pumping fist, her choked scream the sweetest sound I've ever heard. In a powerful surge I bury myself deep, filling every inch of her sweet pussy and coming so hard that it feels as if I'm emptying my soul into her welcoming depths.

When her shudders ease, my mouth finds hers again, and I roll us over so that she's splayed bonelessly on top of me. For a long time we lay there wordlessly, until with a contented sigh, she lifts her head. With her bottom lip pinched between her teeth, she studies my face, her fingers lightly tracing the line of my jaw.

My gaze narrows on that trapped lip. "What?"

"I was just thinking about my Secret Santa." Her eyes gleam with amusement. "And how his Christmas tree was worth *way* more than ten dollars," she tells me, then shrieks with laughter when I immediately toss her onto her back again.

With a growl, I rise over her sexy body as it's still quivering with laughter. Swiftly I replace the condom before pushing her thighs wide and settling between them, my cock pressing against her entrance. "You've got your tree. So tell Santa what you want now, baby."

Giggling, she wraps her legs around me again. "A really big Yule log?"

So Santa gives one to her.

* * *

THIS TIME EMMA WAKES UP before me. She's absent from the bed when I open my eyes, so I slide out from beneath the sweltering mound of blankets and haul on my jeans before blearily making my way into the bathroom. I'm in the middle of a piss when I realize my dick's not shriveling away from the kiss of freezing air. Emma turned up the heat.

I sure as hell hope she didn't do it for me.

Frowning, I finish up and make my way out of the bedroom. The scent of brewing coffee is overpowering the fragrance of her Christmas tree, but I don't find her in the kitchen. Instead she's sitting on the floor of her living room.

Crying.

My heart rips right out of my chest. And I must make a sound—probably like I'm fucking dying—because she turns to look at me, and I see I've made some assumptions again.

She *is* crying. But she's smiling, too.

"You okay, baby?" My voice is raw. Because she's smiling, but my heart is still recovering.

"Yes." Laughing, she wipes away her tears. Or tries to, because more just spill over. "Every column is in the black."

Frowning, I try to make sense of that and can't. "What?"

She waves her hand toward the laptop open on the floor in front of her—then she picks up a slip of paper. A check.

"The bonus," she says and starts choking up again. "It

was five *thousand* dollars."

Oh yeah. It's been a damned good year for the company, which means a damned good year for all of us.

The best year so far. Though I haven't even looked at mine yet.

Reaching into my back pocket, I pull out the crumpled envelope I stuck there last night.

On a strangled gasp, Emma closes her eyes. "Oh my god, you left it in your *pocket?*"

"Yeah."

Where else should I put it? Hell, there's nowhere else to put it now, so after a peek at the amount, I shove it back in.

She moans a little. "A check like that in your back pocket. How many years have you been working there?"

"Ten, officially. But I've been getting bonuses since Dad sold my first design."

She slits one eye open and peers at me through it. "So how long?"

"I'm on fourteen years."

Her eyes close again. "Holy shit."

Yeah, it's a nice little chunk of change. A sweet cherry on top of the design commissions I receive for the custom pieces and catalog sales.

Laughing with disbelief, she shakes her head. "Marianne said your dad puts in a percentage of profits and splits that between employees based on length of time. I figured it would be two to five percent. But this…" Her gaze goes distant for a long second, as if she's calcu[ ] in her head, then surprise widens her eyes. "He must give away half his profits."

"He does." I sink onto the floor beside her. "My mom helped him start up, way back when. She put up half the money. So he gives her fifty percent back to the employees — says he'd never be where he was without someone's generosity."

A smile curves her soft pink lips. "Neither would I."

Maybe a lot of us wouldn't be. I glance at her computer, frowning when I see the spreadsheet. "Now what's this? You didn't bring work home, did you?"

"No. It's my household budget."

I *knew* she'd have something like that. Grinning, I ask, "You track everything?"

"Everything. I even keep a food inventory." Sudden excitement lights her eyes. "Let me take you to breakfast. I can take someone out to breakfast! So let me."

I love seeing her this happy. "All right," I tell her. "But that someone you take to breakfast better always be me."

Laughing, she leans forward to press a kiss to my lips, as if I've done her a favor by agreeing to be taken out. "And I can go get a battery today." Her expression dims a little. "Oh, except it's Christmas Eve. I guess an auto shop might not be able to fit me in."

"You can buy one," I tell her. "I'll put it in for you."

"But —"

"And you'll let me." I stop her before she can protest.

"I'd do the same for Marianne or my dad, all right? It doesn't make any sense for you to pay a mechanic to install a battery when I'm right here with nothing better to do."

"All right." Her face brightens again. "But can we do it first thing after breakfast? We should also stop by the bank right away because they're probably closing early. Then I'll need to be alone the rest of the day."

Alone? I eye her suspiciously. "What are you planning?"

"I can't tell." She grins at me impishly and it's fucking adorable. "It's a secret."

"All right." I might do a few secret things myself—such as take another trip to the jewelry store.

I bought her a ring this week…but there's no need to rush this. I've been worrying that if I didn't grab onto her, she'd run away. So I charged in like a rutting bull moose, as if I've got one chance to claim a cow I've sniffed out.

But rushing isn't what Emma needs. As soon as I found out she was a virgin, I slowed everything way down. I should have done the same while building this relationship between us. Because I ended up taking better care of her pussy than I did with her heart, and I hurt her when I jumped to conclusions, started making assumptions.

And she's been living on the edge for so long, that now she's crying with happiness simply at the thought of having a few solid months ahead of her. Solid months that she earned on her own, not owed to anyone. She doesn't need someone charging in and throwing her off balance again. Better to be someone who is steady and solid at her side.

And she's here with me now. She knows my intentions and that doesn't scare her away. This thing with her, we can do bit by bit. We have the rest of our lives ahead of us.

So it's time to stop being a rutting bull moose and to start being a fucking *man*.

But that doesn't mean I won't be screwing her into oblivion as often as I can.

Gripping her hips, I lift her over onto my lap, facing me. "How you feeling? Sore?"

Her cheeks go pink. "Not *too* sore."

"So at least a little sore." Which means we wait for now. "And definitely not ready for a pounding."

Her lips plump out in a little pout. "Maybe not that."

"We'll hold off on that another day, then." Softly I kiss her before drawing back to ask, "Are you staying with me tonight? And going with me to my dad's tomorrow?"

"Yes and yes."

This time I kiss her long and slow, until she gently pulls away, but she doesn't go far. Instead she looks down at me with new tears in her eyes. But they aren't the tears of despair I remember—or the tears of joy from only minutes ago.

Instead her eyes are filled with hope.

NINE
Emma

ON CHRISTMAS MORNING, I WAKE up to Logan's head between my legs again—but this time he's playing evil Santa, because he works me right up to the edge of an orgasm, then abruptly backs off the bed and pulls me to my feet.

Then I'm standing there with my pussy dripping and my body shaking with need as he drapes a red velvet robe around my shoulders. As soon as he's got the belt tied, he steps into a pair of flannel pajama pants, but he's not being any nicer to himself than he is to me. His huge erection pushes so hard against the front of the pajamas that the waistband is pulling away from the ridged muscles of his abdomen.

Grinning, he drops a kiss to my lips. "Time to open

our presents."

I know exactly where my Christmas present is. I reach for his cock, but he laughs and grabs my hand, pulling me toward the loft's tree. Last night, there were only two presents beneath it — the one I brought for him, and another that he said was from his Secret Santa and that he hadn't opened yet. Now there are three more small boxes, one with my name scrawled across the gold wrapping paper in familiar black marker, and the other two marked with his name, written by the same hand.

I laugh. "Looks like you've been a good boy this year."

"Hell yeah, I have."

He kneels in front of the tree and pulls me down to the floor with him, and I can't recall ever having so much fun on Christmas morning. Even the needy ache of my body just heightens the overall anticipation as he places the box marked with my name on my lap. Then he reaches for the gift I brought, and his biceps flex as he drags the heavy box out from beneath the branches.

Feeling as if the entire world is bright and shiny, I meet his icy blue eyes. He looks just as eager to open his as I am to open mine. "So do we open carefully or rip it all off?"

His answer is to tear the wrapping paper around his box to shreds.

Laughing, I do the same to the pretty gold paper, then my heart stops when I reveal the gift underneath, the red box stamped with the jeweler's signature.

"Oh my god," I whisper and carefully open the box. A large diamond pendant is nestled upon a bed of black velvet. Glittering beneath the colorful lights of the Christmas tree, symmetrical rays of diamond chips set between six larger gems form a stunning snowflake dangling on a platinum chain.

I raise my stunned gaze to Logan's, who has stopped opening his gift to watch my reaction.

"No haggling," he says softly.

"I wasn't going to." My throat is thick. "Will you put it on me?"

His eyes darken as I turn slightly away, lifting my hair from the back of my neck and watching him over my shoulder. His hands are so big, scarred and callused after years of building, yet his fingers so sensitive. He deftly opens a clasp that I would have fumbled over forever.

He moves closer behind me, until I can feel the heat of his body. As the pendant settles into the hollow of my throat, I whisper huskily, "Thank you."

His response is a warm kiss against my nape. My eyes are burning when I turn back, my throat a solid lump.

"All right?" he asks gruffly.

When I nod, he bends his head and kisses me softly before drawing back.

"Now I'm going to see what's in that box. Because it's so damn heavy, I'm guessing you filled it with coal."

I laugh, shaking my head, my hand going to the unfamiliar weight of the pendant lying against my throat. My heart seems to clench tighter as he rips away the final strip of packing tape holding the box closed.

A grin widens his mouth when he looks in at the assortment of books inside. "So I get to judge you now?"

"Yes." A nervous giggle shakes through me. "It's twenty of my favorites — well, twenty of my top fifty, maybe, because you own a lot of my favorites already. So I didn't buy any repeats."

"Are there any of those dirty ones in here?"

My cheeks heat. "Quite a few."

"Hell yeah. I'm going to read those first." Then his voice deepens when he glances at me. "You're already filling up the shelves in your library, baby."

My heart gives a heavy thump. "And you look really angry now."

His icy gaze hardens. "By now you know what this face means."

"Yeah, I do." And my pussy's aching again, my skin tight with anticipation.

On a low growl he says, "Then you open those other two gifts, baby. And I'll give your sweet pussy the hard fucking it's been waiting for."

Breathing slow and heavy, I look to the remaining gifts. There are three left: his present from his Secret Santa and the two others marked with his name.

Reaching under the tree, he tosses the gold-wrapped gifts to me. "They're for me, baby. But you might as well open them, since you'll be the one wearing them."

Clutching them in my lap, I say breathlessly, "Your Secret Santa gift first."

Because I've got a feeling that as soon as we open these, we won't be getting to that one for a while.

Logan seems to agree. Almost impatiently he tears the wrapping from the gift, then abruptly freezes, staring at what he just revealed. The strangled noise he makes almost makes my heart stop, then I realize— It's a laugh. He's choking on a laugh. Because he's laughing so deep and so hard that he's not even making a sound, but his eyes are watering, and his head's bowed as his shoulders shake uncontrollably.

And I can't even figure out what the gift is. There's no packaging—just a short black corrugated tube with smooth cylinders attached to each end. It looks to me like some weird alien sex toy…which might account for his reaction.

"What is it?"

Dragging in a deep breath, he regains some control. He wipes his eyes, then takes another deep breath before he tells me in a strained voice, "It's a bull moose call."

I frown. And that's from his Secret Santa? "What's it used for?"

Another shudder of laughter shakes through him. "When you blow it, you sound like a bull moose. It's usually used for hunting."

Oh. "So you hunt moose?"

"No." Grinning, he puts the moose call aside and his

gaze drops to the gifts on my lap. "Now your turn. The square one, first."

There's a square, and a rectangle. Setting aside the second, I carefully begin to pick at the tape, gently peeling back the folds of wrapping paper at the end.

Logan growls. "Rip it open."

He's not the only evil Santa. Deliberately teasing, I gingerly begin to pick at the tape closing the opposite end.

Abruptly he reaches for me, strong fingers catching my chin. Expression hard, eyes glittering, he says in a soft voice, "As soon as those are open and you're wearing them, I'm going to put you on your knees and get my thick cock into you as deep and as hard as I can."

Oh god. I rip the package open, my hands shaking with the force of the need raging through me.

A pair of silk stockings in red and white stripes. They're longer than my knee-high socks, with a lacy band around the top.

"Now put those on." Logan watches me, his big hand stroking the bulge of his cock through his flannel pants. "Let me see those stripes go all the way up those long, sexy legs."

Not all the way up. Just to mid-thigh, where the elasticized lace holds them in place. They're soft and feel deliciously luxurious against my skin, so despite my desperate need I take my time, pointing my toes and rolling each one slowly over my knee and up the length of my thigh.

Logan's teeth are gritted, a muscle flexing in his jaw by the time I've finished. "Now the other gift."

I don't hesitate before opening this one: a sleep mask, made of the softest velvet in a deep, cherry red.

A red velvet that matches the robe I'm wearing. He'd given me another gift without my even realizing it.

My breath shuddering through parted lips, I slip the mask over my head. The last thing I see is Logan, watching me with ravenous hunger burning in his icy gaze, his big hand stroking the thick length of his cock.

"Stand up now, baby."

His soft growl is already closer. Muscles trembling, I rise to my feet. Immediately there's a tug at my waist—Logan loosening the belt of my robe. The heavy material gapes open at the front and prickles of excitement race over my skin. Then callused palms glide over my shoulders, pushing at the sleeves, and with a whisper of crumpling velvet the robe falls to the floor.

Leaving me clad only in my stockings, the diamond pendant, and my mask. I stand shivering, knowing Logan's looking at me wearing nothing but the gifts he just gave to me.

"You're so fucking beautiful, Emma." His harsh voice comes from directly in front of me. "I could just look at you forever. But you want more than that, don't you?"

So much more. "Yes," I whisper.

"I'll give it to you, baby."

Without warning, strong arms sweep me up against

a broad chest. I gasp, then his mouth finds mine as he carries me — to the bed, where he gently sets me down, my head supported by a soft pillow.

But his hands on my hips aren't gentle. They're firm and unyielding as he rolls me over onto my stomach.

"Up on your knees, Emma," comes his rough command. "Elbows on the bed, legs spread."

With my bottom high in the air and my sex exposed to his gaze. Face flaming behind the mask, I get my knees under me, my pussy feeling swollen and wet and so needy.

Because I'm already ready, I realize. Because he worked me up so far, then left me hanging, stewing in my need as we opened the gifts.

Evil Santa. Planning this all along.

And that's so damn hot.

The rip of a condom wrapper is followed by the dip of the mattress beneath his weight. I bite my lip as long fingers slick through the folds of my pussy.

A rough groan sounds behind me. "So hot and wet. You going to take everything I have to give, baby?"

"Yes," I reply, then begin shaking in anticipation as the blunt head of his cock lodges firmly at my entrance.

"Push back, Emma." His voice is hoarse with need. "If you want what I have to give you, then you need to take it first."

Oh god. Rising up on my hands, I press back, seeking that incredible sensation of being filled. But there's only pressure, so much pressure.

"I'm big, baby." Each word sounds tortured. "You've got to push harder."

To take the thick head of his cock. I can picture that flared crown, remember the feel and taste of it beneath my tongue. And now the stretch of my delicate flesh around it as I push back harder. Suddenly he breaches my entrance, that broad head lodged just inside me, the ecstasy of taking him overwhelming every other feeling.

With a soft cry, I collapse onto my elbows again as hard hands grip my hips.

"Ah, Emma." Raw and deep, his voice is pure gravel, pure emotion. "Look at the way you give yourself to me. I'm so crazy fucking in love with you."

And even as that pleasure washes through me, with one slick thrust, he buries his cock deep. So deep I can barely breathe, then he fucks hard into me again and I scream against my pillow, my hands fisting as I'm bombarded with sensations, my breasts jolting with every sharp thrust, my nipples on fire, my pussy full, so full, the slap of our skin so wet and the rhythm so fast.

Cock pounding into me, Logan's fingers tangle in my hair and he pulls me back harder, fucks deeper. "You like this, baby?"

"Yes." It's a breathless, sobbing cry. "It's so good."

His groaning laugh is followed by, "*Too* good, baby. I'm not going to last. So we need to make you feel even better."

Releasing my hair, his hand slips between my legs. The stroke of his fingers across my over-sensitized clit is like an electric shock, searing every nerve inside me, the sharp pleasure of his thrusting cock suddenly too much, too much, but he's fucking me deep and hard and fast, my pussy clenching around him, his fingers delivering another slick jolt to my clit and then I'm coming, screaming as my inner muscles clamp down on his thick shaft, clutching him tight even as he shoves hard into me a final time. He abruptly stills, and the heavy pulse of his erection deep inside me makes me shudder in ecstasy again.

I collapse forward and Logan comes with me, his weight heavy but I love it, love the sweaty press of his hair-roughened chest against my back, the fullness of his softening cock still inside me.

Then he mutters, "The fucking condom," and I moan when he gently withdraws. He disappears into the bathroom and returns a moment later, sliding into bed and pulling me against his side.

Utterly wrung out, I manage to mumble, "This is the best Christmas ever."

His huff of laughter sounds like wry agreement, but a moment later he says, "I bet next year is even better."

I won't bet against that. I rise up on my elbow, looking down at him, and my heart is so full and happy that I don't know what else this could be. "Are you ready to catch me?"

Abruptly he sits up, framing my face in his hands. "Are you falling?"

Overwhelmed by the emotion, tears burn my eyes. "So hard."

"I'm right here, baby." His voice is hoarse, his icy gaze searching mine. "I always will be."

I can see that, too. So clearly. *Always.*

So I give him everything I can.

"I love you, Logan Crenshaw." My heart in my throat, I wreath my arms around his shoulders, holding him close. "I am so crazy fucking in love with you."

And his beautiful grin in response, his fierce kiss—they're the sweetest gifts I could ever imagine.

EPILOGUE
Logan

ONE YEAR LATER

I FIND EMMA IN THE LIBRARY, stretched out on her belly on the chaise longue in front of the fireplace. A short stack of books is sitting on the floor next to the chaise — the books she received at my dad's house today.

There are plenty more books scattered around the room, waiting to be shelved. She finally gave up her apartment and moved into my house three months ago, and the last time I saw her spreadsheet, the rent line was empty and a book budget had taken its place. So she's filling those shelves with books faster than she can read them.

And it's easy to see what happened here. She was just putting the books away, she said. But she probably opened one and got caught up, losing track of time — and if she's truly engrossed, she becomes completely oblivious to anything happening around her.

It's just another thing I've discovered about her in the past year. Just another thing that I love about her.

I knew Emma Williams was right for me the second I met her. But I had no idea how much I'd love her when I finally got to know her.

I didn't know I'd ever love anyone this much.

And she's so deep in her book, she doesn't realize I'm there until my fingers are sliding up the backs of her long, long legs. She's wearing a swingy little skirt again, different from the one she was wearing last year when I met her, but just as capable of driving me out of my fucking mind.

"Shhhhh," I tell her when she tries to roll onto her side. "Keep reading. And stay quiet."

"Why?" she whispers.

"Because you don't want Logan walking in and seeing Santa pushing this skirt up over your ass."

A little giggle shakes through her. "You're my Secret Santa?"

"Yes."

"Are you going to give me something, Santa?"

My voice deepens to a growl. "I'm going to take something, baby. But don't make any sound. Because the man who loves you feels like he's got big fucking holes in his chest when you're not cuddled up next to him. So he might come looking for you."

"That would be bad," she whispers. "If he came in and Santa was giving me a really big Christmas tree."

I can't stop my laugh. Christ, I love this woman. So much.

Her breath shudders as my fingers slick between her thighs. She's already so hot and wet, I'll be able to slide into her so fucking easy. But that's not the plan.

Not yet.

"Your pussy's begging for my thick cock, baby. But before I give it to you, you've got one more present to open."

This time when she turns onto her side, I let her. Her brown eyes narrow at me. "What is it?"

Just a small gift. But I've had it for a year. Now it's in the palm of my hand, ready to slip onto her finger.

But first, I give her a note. Her gaze widens as she begins to read.

> *Open the box.*
> *Put on the ring.*
> *Say you'll marry me.*
> LOGAN

She looks up with me, eyes shining with tears of joy and hope.

And with a single word, she gives me everything.

Made in the USA
Las Vegas, NV
01 December 2024